T0278480

THE
EERIE BOOK

THE
EERIE BOOK

EDITED BY
MARGARET ARMOUR

ILLUSTRATIONS BY
W.B. MACDOUGALL

INTRODUCTION BY
KIRSTY LOGAN

BODLEIAN
LIBRARY
PUBLISHING

This edition first published in 2024 by Bodleian Library Publishing
Broad Street, Oxford OX1 3BG
www.bodleianshop.co.uk

ISBN 978 1 85124 640 3

Introduction © Kirsty Logan, 2024

This expanded edition
© Bodleian Library Publishing, University of Oxford, 2024

Illustrations by W.B. Macdougall.
University of California Libraries, YRL Collection 1605

All rights reserved.

First published in 1898 by J. Shiells & Co., London

This book was first published in the 1890s.
It reflects the views and attitudes of the period.

No part of this book may be reproduced, stored in a retrieval system, or
transmitted in any form or by any means, electronic, mechanical, photocopying,
recording, or otherwise, without the written permission of the Bodleian Library,
except for the purpose of research or private study, or criticism or review.

Publisher: Samuel Fanous
Managing Editor: Susie Foster
Editor: Janet Phillips
Picture Editor: Leanda Shrimpton
Cover design by Dot Little at the Bodleian Library
Designed and typeset by Lucy Morton of illuminati in 11 on 15 Caslon
Printed and bound in China by C&C Offset Printing Co., Ltd.
on 120 gsm Chinese Baijin Pure woodfree paper

British Library Catalogue in Publishing Data
A CIP record of this publication is available from the British Library

CONTENTS

INTRODUCTION

by Kirsty Logan

W E HAVE ALWAYS BEEN HAUNTED. We will always be haunted. We love—*love*—to be haunted.

We love to slip out of the street light and into the shadows of the alley, to lift up the grimiest rock to see what's crawling underneath, to slow down and try to glimpse something red in the flashing blue lights of the ambulance at the side of the road. We're creepy, and we like to be creeped out. And by 'we' I of course mean me, but possibly you too, otherwise you wouldn't have picked up this book.

THE BOOK

The Eerie Book is a collection of supernatural stories ranging from gory folk and fairy tales to Gothic short stories, to extracts of classic novels. At least one of the pieces included will likely be familiar, though there will be something new too.

The interest in this particular book, for me, is the curation: the way that the stories are put in conversation with one another. I've read ghost stories and I've read fairy tales, but there's something interesting about making them stand beside one another, in making them look one another in the eye and try to find a common language.

The Kuleshov effect, named for Russian film-maker Lev Kuleshov in the 1920s, is a film-editing effect where viewers derive more meaning from the interaction of two sequential shots than from a single shot in isolation. The Kuleshov effect is also applicable to texts: the way that one story leads—or bleeds—into the next gives it a different meaning than it would if read in isolation.

The Eerie Book begins with Poe's "Masque of the Red Death"—uncomfortably appropriate here in our post-pandemic world—with the image of "the redness and the horror of blood" and ending in the "blood-bedewed halls". From blood to blood—so when the next tale begins with the protagonist cheerily strolling forth to enjoy the sea breeze, do we expect anything other than gore and gloom to await him? And, of course, through a journey of mysterious bells and strange windows, the story ends in "agonising screams and shrieks" of the tortured. It's almost a relief when the next story, horribly, is "The Mother and the Dead Child". The child is already dead; how much worse could it get, we ask? The book surprises us again, as instead of a Gothic gore-fest we get a poignant and melancholic tale of loss.

I imagine these stories all in a queue outside a door, some kind of vague and sinister doctor's office perhaps, each story waiting its turn, shoulders bumping, hearing one another's shoe-shuffling and throat-clearing, eyeing each other up. Catching the scent of nervous sweat, perhaps, or a forgotten shred of meat beneath a thumbnail, spying a spot of blood on a sleeve.

Aren't they gory little delights, these stories? How they chafe when confined together; how they blossom and bleed.

The Author

Margaret Armour was a Scottish writer born in 1860 in Abercorn, a village close to the Firth of Forth, just west of Edinburgh. When she compiled *The Eerie Book* she was, by pleasant coincidence, the same age as I am now. Her taste for the Gothic, the melancholic and the dramatic can be gleaned from the titles of two of her poetry collections: *Songs of Love and Death* (1896) and *The Shadow of Love* (1898). Adoration and attachment; destruction and darkness.

She was also a translator; she translated the *Nibelungenlied*, an epic poem written around 1200 in Middle High German, into English, in what she termed "plain prose". This was published in 1897 as *The Fall of the Nibelungs*, and was later included in the Everyman's Library. She revisited these characters and world later when she translated Richard Wagner's cycle of four German-language operas (or *Musikdrama*, as Wagner called them), *The Ring of the Nibelung*, as well as the German medieval epic *Gudrun*. (An aside: the word 'eerie' is Germanic in origin.)

But before all that, she published her first book, *The Home and Early Haunts of Robert Louis Stevenson* (1895). If there's anything that I think ties all the stories in *The Eerie Book* together, it's those: homes and hauntings. We can't know what kind of place home was for Margaret Armour, but I like to think it was as operatic, mysterious and inspirational as the stories she collected—and as the illustrations her husband created for *The Eerie Book*.

THE ILLUSTRATOR

William Brown (credited as W.B.) Macdougall's style has strong echoes of Aubrey Beardsley; the images are symbolic and sombre. I've spent much time lost in the image on the cover of *The Eerie Book*, and every time I revisit it the figure seems to change.

First, she's a predator: a hag, a fairy-tale witch in her black cape and pointed hat, cavorting animalistically and barefoot through the woods to curse someone. Is that a fox's tail streaming out behind her? Is she ensuring that her familiar is following, its maw reddened with a fresh kill?

Then I look again and she's all victim: a maiden, eyes wide in fear as she flees from an unknown pursuer, her long blonde hair whipping in the storm of pathetic fallacy. (Witch or maiden, after all, are the only things a woman can be.)

What I like best about the image is that she's enveloped in black: she's shapeless, unembodied, revealing little more than a firm ankle and enormous eyes. Look, she seems to say. Look at me. Follow me. Horrors await, and you'll love them.

We loved tales of blood and death a century ago when this book was first published; we loved them for centuries before that. I expect we will love them for centuries still to come. We may think we're different now. We have different beliefs; we tell different stories. We are haunted by different fears.

But one thing that never seems to change about humans is that desire to slip out of the light and into the shadows; to lift up the rock; to stare at the ambulance lights. In another hundred years we will crave stories of new horrors—or perhaps these same old classic ones. As the final story in this book says: "the secret passages still survive".

Let's descend the darkened stairs together. Let's follow the witch into the woods. Let's see what we find in those old hidden passages.

THE MASQUE
OF THE RED DEATH

T HE "RED DEATH" had long devastated the country. No pestilence had ever been so fatal or so hideous. Blood was its Avator and its seal—the redness and the horror of blood. There were sharp pains, and sudden dizziness, and then profuse bleeding at the pores, with dissolution. The scarlet stains upon the body, and especially upon the face of the victim, were the pest ban which shut him out from the aid and from the sympathy of his fellow-men; and the whole seizure, progress, and termination of the disease were the incidents of half-an-hour.

But the Prince Prospero was happy and dauntless and sagacious. When his dominions were half-depopulated, he summoned to his presence a thousand hale and light-hearted friends from among the knights and dames of his court, and with these retired to the deep seclusion of one of his castellated abbeys. This was an extensive and magnificent structure, the creation of the prince's own eccentric yet august taste. A strong and lofty wall girdled it in. This wall had gates of iron. The courtiers, having entered, brought furnaces and massy hammers and welded the bolts. They resolved to leave means neither of ingress nor egress to the sudden impulses of despair from without or of frenzy from within. The abbey was amply provisioned. With such precautions the courtiers might bid defiance to contagion. The external world could take care of itself. In the meantime it was folly to grieve or to think. The prince had provided all the appliances of pleasure. There were buffoons, there were improvisatori, there were ballet-dancers, there were musicians, there was beauty, there was wine. All these and security were within. Without was the "Red Death".

It was toward the close of the fifth or sixth month of his seclusion, and while the pestilence raged most furiously abroad, that the Prince Prospero entertained his thousand friends at a masked ball of the most unusual magnificence.

It was a voluptuous scene that masquerade. But first let me tell of the rooms in which it was held. There were seven—an imperial suite. In many palaces, however, such suites form a long and straight vista, while the folding doors slide back nearly to the walls on either hand, so that the view of the whole extent is scarcely impeded. Here the case was very different, as might have been expected from the duke's love of the bizarre. The apartments were so irregularly disposed that the vision embraced but little more than one at a time. There was a sharp turn at every twenty or thirty yards, and at each turn a novel effect. To the right and left, in the middle of each wall, a tall and narrow Gothic window looked out upon a closed corridor which pursued the windings of the suite. These windows were of stained glass whose colour varied in accordance with the prevailing hue of the decorations of the chamber into which it opened. That at the eastern extremity was hung, for example, in blue, and vividly blue were its windows. The second chamber was purple in its ornaments and tapestries, and here the panes were purple. The third was green throughout, and so were the casements. The fourth was furnished and lighted with orange, the fifth with white, the sixth with violet. The seventh apartment was closely shrouded in black velvet tapestries that hung all over the ceiling and down the walls, falling in heavy folds upon a carpet of the same material and hue. But in this chamber only the colour of the windows failed to correspond with the decorations.

The panes here were scarlet—a deep blood-colour. Now in no one of the seven apartments was there any lamp or candelabrum amid the profusion of golden ornaments that lay scattered to and fro or depended from the roof. There was no light of any kind emanating from lamp or candle within the suite of chambers; but in the corridors that followed the suite there stood opposite to each window a heavy tripod bearing a brazier of fire that projected its rays through the tinted glass and so glaringly illumined the room. And thus were produced a multitude of gaudy and fantastic appearances. But in the western or black chamber the effect of the fire-light that streamed upon the dark hangings, through the blood-tinted panes, was ghastly in the extreme, and produced so wild a look upon the countenances of those who entered that there were few of the company bold enough to set foot within its precincts at all.

It was in this apartment also that there stood against the western wall a gigantic clock of ebony. Its pendulum swung to and fro with a dull, heavy, monotonous clang; and when the minute-hand made the circuit of the face, and the hour was to be stricken, there came from the brazen lungs of the clock a sound which was clear and loud and deep and exceedingly musical, but of so peculiar a note and emphasis that, at each lapse of an hour, the musicians of the orchestra were constrained to pause momentarily in their performance to hearken to the sound; and thus the waltzers perforce ceased their evolutions, and there was a brief disconcert of the whole gay company, and while the chimes of the clock yet rang it was observed that the giddiest grew pale, and the more aged and sedate passed their hands over their brows as if in confused reverie or meditation: but when the echoes had fully ceased, a light laughter at once pervaded the assembly; the musicians looked at each other and smiled as if at their own nervousness and

4

folly, and made whispering vows each to the other that the next chiming of the clock should produce in them no similar emotion, and then, after the lapse of sixty minutes (which embrace three thousand and six hundred seconds of the time that flies), there came yet another chiming of the clock, and then were the same disconcert and tremulousness and meditation as before.

But in spite of these things it was a gay and magnificent revel. The tastes of the duke were peculiar. He had a fine eye for colours and effects. He disregarded the decora of mere fashion. His plans were bold and fiery, and his conceptions glowed with barbaric lustre. There are some who would have thought him mad. His followers felt that he was not. It was necessary to hear, and see, and touch him to be sure that he was not.

He had directed, in great part, the movable embellishments of the seven chambers, upon occasion of this great fête; and it was his own guiding taste which had given character to the masqueraders. Be sure they were grotesque. There were much glare and glitter and piquancy and phantasm—much of what has been since seen in "Hernani". There were arabesque figures with unsuited limbs and appointments. There were delirious fancies such as the madman fashions. There were much of the beautiful, much of the wanton, much of the bizarre, something of the terrible, and not a little of that which might have excited disgust. To and fro in the seven chambers there stalked, in fact, a multitude of dreams. And these—the dreams—writhed in and about, taking hue from the rooms, and causing the wild music of the orchestra to seem as the echo of their steps. And, anon there strikes the ebony clock which stands in the hall of the velvet; and then, for a moment, all is still, and all is silent save the voice of the clock. The dreams are stiff-frozen as they stand. But the echoes of the chime die away—they have endured but an instant—and a light, half-subdued laughter floats after them as they depart. And now again the music swells, and the dreams live, and writhe to and fro more merrily than ever, taking hue from the many tinted windows through which stream the rays from the tripods. But to the chamber which lies most eastwardly of the seven, there are now none of the maskers who venture; for the night is waning away; and there flows a ruddier light through the blood-coloured panes; and the blackness of the sable drapery appals; and to him whose foot falls upon the sable carpet, there comes from the near clock of ebony a muffled peal more solemnly emphatic than any which reaches their ears who indulge in the more remote gaieties of the other apartments.

But these other apartments were densely crowded, and in them beat feverishly the heart of life. And the revel went whirlingly on, until at length there commenced the sounding of midnight upon the clock. And then the music ceased, as I have told; and the evolutions of the waltzers were quieted; and there was an uneasy cessation of all things as before. But now there were twelve strokes to be sounded by the bell of the clock; and thus it happened, perhaps, that more of thought crept, with more of time, into the meditations of the thoughtful among those who revelled. And thus, too, it happened, perhaps, that before the last echoes of the last chime had utterly sunk into silence, there were many individuals in the crowd who had found leisure to become aware of the presence of a masked figure which had arrested the attention of no single individual before. And the rumour of this new presence having spread itself whisperingly around, there arose at length from the whole company a buzz, or murmur, expressive of disapprobation and surprise—then, finally, of terror, of horror, and of disgust.

In an assembly of phantasms such as I have painted, it may well be supposed that no ordinary appearance could have excited such sensation. In truth, the masquerade licence of the night was nearly unlimited; but the figure in question had out-Heroded Herod, and gone beyond the bounds of even the prince's indefinite decorum. There are chords in the hearts of the most reckless which cannot be touched without emotion. Even with the utterly lost, to whom life and death are equally jests, there are matters of which no jest can be made. The whole company indeed seemed now deeply to feel that in the costume and bearing of the stranger neither wit nor propriety existed. The figure was tall and gaunt, and shrouded from head to foot in the habiliments of the grave. The mask which concealed the visage was made so nearly to resemble the countenance of a stiffened corpse that the closest scrutiny must have had difficulty in detecting the cheat. And yet all this might have been endured, if not approved, by the mad revellers around. But the mummer had gone so far as to assume the type of the Red Death. His vesture was dabbled in blood—and his broad brow, with all the features of the face, was besprinkled with the scarlet horror.

When the eyes of Prince Prospero fell upon this spectral image (which, with a slow and solemn movement, as if more fully to sustain its rôle, stalked to and fro among the waltzers), he was seen to be convulsed in the first moment with a strong shudder either of terror or distaste; but in the next his brow reddened with rage.

"Who dares?" he demanded hoarsely of the courtiers who stood near him—"who dares insult us with this blasphemous mockery? Seize him and unmask him, that we may know whom we have to hang at sunrise from the battlements!"

It was in the eastern or blue chamber in which stood the Prince Prospero as he uttered these words. They rang throughout the seven rooms loudly and clearly—for the prince was a bold and robust man, and the music had become hushed at the waving of his hand.

It was in the blue room where stood the prince, with a group of pale courtiers by his side. At first, as he spoke, there was a slight rushing movement of this group in the direction of the intruder, who at the moment was also near at hand, and now, with deliberate and stately step, made closer approach to the speaker. But, from a certain nameless awe with which the mad assumptions of the mummer had inspired the whole party, there were found none who put forth hand to seize him; so that unimpeded he passed within a yard of the prince's person; and while the vast assembly, as if with one impulse, shrank from the centres of the rooms to the walls, he made his way uninterruptedly, but with the same solemn and measured step which had distinguished him from the first, through the blue chamber to the purple—through the purple to the green—through the green to the orange—through this again to the white and even thence to the violet, ere a decided movement had been made to arrest him. It was then, however, that the Prince Prospero, maddening with rage and the shame of his own momentary cowardice, rushed hurriedly through the six chambers, while none followed him on account of a deadly terror that had seized upon all. He bore aloft a drawn dagger, and had approached in rapid impetuosity, to within three or four feet of the retreating figure, when the latter, having attained the extremity of the velvet apartment, turned suddenly and confronted his pursuer. There was a sharp cry—and the dagger dropped gleaming upon the sable carpet, upon which, instantly afterwards, fell prostrate in death the Prince Prospero. Then, summoning the wild courage of despair, a throng of the revellers at once threw themselves into the black apartment, and, seizing the mummer, whose tall figure stood erect and motionless within the shadow of the ebony clock, gasped in unutterable horror at finding the grave cerements and corpse-like mask which they handled with so violent a rudeness, untenanted by any tangible form.

And now was acknowledged the presence of the Red Death. He had come like a thief in the night; and one by one dropped the revellers in the blood-bedewed halls of their revel, and died each in the despairing posture of his fall; and the life of the ebony clock went out with that of the last of the gay; and the flames of the tripods expired; and the darkness and decay and the Red Death held illimitable dominion over all.

THE IRON COFFIN

O TTO PIANALLA HAD STROLLED FORTH, shortly after sunset, from the house in which the shipwrecked party had been lodged by order of the Duke of Ferrara; and he bent his steps towards the shore to enjoy the refreshing breeze which the wings of the evening wafted over the deep blue waters of the Adriatic.

He was standing in a contemplative mood, upon a low reef which jutted out into the sea, when the sounds of footsteps fell upon his ears. He looked back, and beheld three men advancing towards him.

Not suspecting treachery, he again turned his eyes upon the broad expanse which lay at his feet, and in whose bosom was now reflected the gem-like lustre of a thousand stars.

But in a few moments he was seized rudely from behind: he attempted to resist—the effort was vain, for his arms were pinioned with cords in an instant;—he demanded the cause of this outrage—and his question elicited no answer.

The three men performed their work in dogged silence.

Having securely bound Otto's arms, they led him away along the seashore for a considerable distance, so as to avoid the outskirts of the town; and at length they turned abruptly into a narrow path which ran through a thick grove situated upon a somewhat steep acclivity.

Otto endeavoured to learn the motive of his arrest: and he appealed to the men to satisfy him upon that head.

But they uttered not a word in reply!

When the uppermost verge of the grove was gained, the black and gloomy towers of the Castle of Solitude were seen at a short distance, standing out in dark relief against the star-lit horizon.

Otto sighed as he beheld that sombre fortress of which he had already heard enough to arouse the worst fears in his mind;—and a tear trembled upon his dark lash as he thought of his wife and children.

Then he reproached himself for giving way to that temporary depression, instead of putting his faith in the supreme power which had so often led him safely through dangers of a menacing and even an appalling nature.

The ominous silence in which his guards thus shrouded themselves was calculated to inspire the prisoner with the most gloomy forebodings; and he prayed inwardly, as he accompanied them along a series of stone passages, lighted only by the lurid glare of the torch—he prayed, to prepare himself for death!

At the end of the last passage which they thus traversed Schurmann opened a low door, which was provided outside with massive bolts, padlocks, and chains.

The cords were now removed from Otto's arms; and he was thrust into the dungeon to which that well-defended door gave admittance.

A moment afterwards, and the ominous clanking of the bolts and chains fell upon his ears.

He sate down on the straw which littered the floor of the dungeon, and, amidst the almost total darkness in which he was plunged, began to meditate sorrowfully upon his condition.

What would his beloved wife and darling children think of his sudden and unaccountable absence? Oh! the idea of their terrible suspense was almost insupportable; and even the virtuous—the heaven-confiding Otto was now reduced to the brink of despair.

And for what fate was he reserved? For death, perhaps! But by what means was his end to be accomplished? Not by sudden violence—not by the bravo's knife;—or else wherefore should his enemies have conveyed him thither? Alas! was famine—was starvation to be his doom? He feared so!

But who were his enemies? Had he only one, or many? He knew that Lucrezia Borgia was the Duchess of Ferrara, and that she was then at the palace of Lissa with the royal court;—but surely—surely she could not be his persecutress?

Had he not saved her brother from a dungeon—at the peril of finding one himself? No—Lucrezia could not be his enemy! And yet—and yet, who would dare to perpetrate this outrage beneath the very eyes, as it were, of the Duke and Duchess to whose rule the island, with its fortress, belonged!

Terrible uncertainty!—bewildering suspense!

As Otto sate, thus ruminating, upon the straw of his cell, his eyes gradually became more accustomed to the obscurity; and a light dawned upon him by very slow degrees, and so faintly that when its presence first struck him he doubted whether it was not an optical delusion.

But, as he gazed—and gazed with straining eyes, he became convinced that there were really windows along the top of that side or wall of the dungeon towards which his face was turned.

Yes—he could now count those windows, guarded with their massive iron bars.

There were five; and they formed a range, separated only from each other by very narrow divisions.

The door was in the side facing the windows.

Otto rose from his straw, and endeavoured to raise himself up to the casements; but they were too high to reach with a spring, and there was not a single projection to break the surface of the wall.

And that wall—and the other walls of the dungeon—oh! there was no possibility of mistaking the nature of the material of which they were made; for as Otto passed his hand over them, the cold touch of iron sent a chill to his very heart's core!

In what kind of a place, then, was he? He examined it more closely with his eyes and hands; and he was speedily struck by the extraordinary shape of that dungeon.

Very long and very narrow, it at first appeared to him a section cut off from a passage by building two partition walls across it; but, no—the side walls were not straight!

More closely—more attentively still did he examine the dungeon; and at last—with his blood curdling in his veins—was he forced to stop at the horrible conviction that the dungeon was built in the shape of a coffin!

Yes: he was enclosed in an iron coffin—at one end of which was the door, and at the other the five windows. "Oh! my beloved wife—my dearest children, am I separated from you for ever?" exclaimed Otto Pianalla, falling upon his knees in the midst of that dungeon of a shape so appallingly foreboding. "Great Father of Mercy, wilt thou make her so soon a widow—and them fatherless so young? But in thee I place my trust: thy will be done!"

Then from his bosom he drew forth a small box of sandalwood, and piously kissed the relic which it contained.

That relic was the wood of the Ark!

Then he lay down, and endeavoured to court slumber; for he was fearful of trusting himself alone with his thoughts. Sleep soon fell upon him; and his dreams were to some extent cheering. The nature of those visions was pervaded by the idea of his confinement in that horrible dungeon; but amidst the gloom of this strange and mysterious immurement, his imagination caught glimpses of hope and scintillations of eventual fecility.

He was thus hovering, in his slumbers, between the sad reality of the present and the brighter anticipations of the future, when the loud crashing sound of a bell awoke him with a terrific start.

That bell appeared to ring upon the very roof of the iron dungeon, the metallic echoes of which responded with a din as if the sides—the floor—and the ceiling vibrated long and perceptibly to the sudden clang.

The bell, however, beat but once; though the humming sound continued to ring for more than a minute in the artist's ear.

It was morning; and the interior of the dungeon was now plainly visible in respect to all the ominous features of its shape. The light that prevailed within was of that dim nature which precedes the sunrise by nearly half-an-hour. Yet the sun has already risen;—but then the windows were so small, the horn of which the panes were made was so dull in hue, and the iron bars were so thick, that even at mid-day no better light could penetrate into that living tomb!

When the first bewildering effects of the sudden clang of the bell had passed away, Otto's eyes wandered round and round the dungeon—as if he could scarcely believe that a portion of what had followed him in his dreams was really true,—as if the horrors of his position had just burst upon him for the first time, in all their appalling forms and colours!

But when he had poured forth his matin-prayer he grew calmer, and then surveyed the dungeon with more tranquil attention.

Glancing first towards the door, he beheld some light object projecting as it were from the middle: he approached that point, and, to his surprise and joy, discovered a small loaf and a pitcher of water standing upon a sort of shelf attached to the door. On a closer examination, he observed that there was a small trap, or wicket, in the door, opening just above the shelf, and by means of which the food had been introduced from outside.

"Heaven be thanked!" cried Otto: "then I am not doomed to die of famine!"

Returning, with the loaf and the jug, to his straw in the middle of the dungeon, the artist sat down, and ate and drank sparingly—for he knew not how long a period might elapse ere the provision would be renewed.

But as his eyes wandered round the horrible place from time to time, he was suddenly startled by a circumstance which he had not before noticed during the half hour that had now elapsed since he was awakened by the bell.

This circumstance was connected with the range of windows. He felt convinced that on the preceding night he had counted five—counted them over and over again,—remarked them, in a word, most attentively!

And now there were but four!

Was this possible? Could he have been deceived on the previous night? or was he deluded now?

He advanced nearer to the wall which contained the windows—nearer to what might be called the head of the coffin;—and, surely enough, there were but four windows!

It was clear, then, that he had been deceived in his computation the night before: at least he thought so!

The four windows formed a range all across the top of the wall; and if there had been originally five, the removal or filling up of one must have caused a blank space somewhere along that range.

But there was no such space—the range was uniform, extending from angle to angle along the head of the coffin!

Oh! how shall we attempt to describe the gloom and weariness—the intervals of soul-crushing thoughts, succeeded by others of prayer and hope—which characterised the passage of that long, long day?

Not a sound from without broke upon the awful silence of the dungeon; not a human voice, nor a human footstep—not even the notes of a bell proclaiming the hour,—no—nor the chirrup of a bird on the ledge of the casements, met the ear of the prisoner!

Night came at last—and he determined to watch at the door of the dungeon, to appeal to the person who might bring him food.

There he took his station, keeping his hand fixed upon the panel of the iron door, to ascertain the moment when the wicket was about to be opened—so fearful was he of losing the opportunity of addressing himself to a human soul.

But hour after hour passed; and no one came:—the panel moved not—his food was not renewed. And yet but a morsel of the loaf and but a drop of the water remained to him!

Wearied with watching—and reduced almost to despair by the thought of his wife and children—and now assailed by the horrible idea that his provisions were to be supplied so scantily and at such distant intervals, that a lingering death of slow famine must be his fate,—Otto Pianalla once more threw himself upon his knees, prayed fervently, and shortly after sank into a deep slumber.

His dreams were again to some degree of a cheering nature; and again were they suddenly and cruelly interrupted by the iron clang of the deafening bell.

But this time it beat twice!

Otto started up, and glanced rapidly round the dungeon—or rather from end to end; for it seemed to have grown narrower!

Yes—and, as he gazed, it also appeared to have become shorter; for the straw in the middle struck him as being nearer to the walls every way.

But food—food!—for he was hungry! And, behold—upon the little shelf projecting from the door were a loaf and another pitcher of water.

"Again do I thank Heaven that famine is not to be my fate!" exclaimed Otto. "But for what purpose am I here? Is it to linger in solitude, until the lonely captivity of long, long years shall hurl my reason from its seat? Oh! death were preferable to that! Ah!—what do I see?"

He uttered these last words with a species of agonising scream—for his eyes had wandered towards the windows, of which there were but three!

Starting from the straw, he hastened to examine the wall in which the windows were set. It was now so narrow that when he stretched out his arms, his hands touched the angles where the sides of the coffin joined the head.

But still the windows—the three remaining windows were uniform as a range: there was no blank space in any part. The sides, then, had grown closer to each other: yes—yes—he could now doubt the fact no longer!

And not only had the windows diminished in number;—they were lower than when he first entered that dreadful place! Still, the top of the range touched the ceiling—touched the lid of the iron coffin!

Could all this be a delusion? Was he already turning mad?

No—no; he was sane—too sane to be deceived any longer as to the appearances which now struck terror to his inmost soul! For on the first night of his captivity, he was unable to reach the bottom of the windows even with a leap;—but at present he could touch the massive iron bars of the casements without so much as standing upon tip-toe.

And the roof—oh! that had become lower: it had descended with the windows!

Horrible ideas flashed to his mind:—those walls would collapse—that roof would descend—and his form was destined to be crushed to atoms in that iron coffin!—Or else the walls and the roof would only approach each other at such a distance, as to form the cell into the precise size, as it was already in the shape, of a coffin, and thus would he be, as it were, buried alive!

Merciful God! was such to be his fate?

Recovering from the first access of despair, Otto Pianalla knelt down, and prayed fervently—fervently—more fervently, if possible, than he had ever yet prayed; and he rose in a state of mind considerably calmed—but, alas! calmed only with that resignation which nerves a good man to meet approaching death.

Wearily, wearily, passed the second day; and the third night arrived.

So overcome with the fatigue of intense meditation was he, that—abandoning the idea of again watching at the wicket—he threw himself upon the straw, and slept profoundly.

But, in his slumbers, a strange vision visited him.

He thought that some being, of undefined shape and mien, appeared to him—there, in that dungeon—and offered him liberty—long life—pleasure—power—happiness of all kinds, upon one condition, which this mysterious, vague, and dream-like visitant hesitated to name. But Otto pressed him to declare the terms on which these boons were offered; for the artist longed to embrace his wife and children again. Then it seemed to him as if the being leant over him, and whispered in his ear words of so terrible—so appalling a nature,—conditions of so fearful a kind,—that he started up wildly, and commanded the fiend to begone. Yet the shade appeared to linger; whereupon Otto instinctively drew forth a holy relic of the Ark, and by that precious symbol of God's mercy adjured the demon to depart.

At that instant the dreadful bell upon the roof sounded, once—twice—thrice!

Otto's senses were so bewildered that for some minutes he knew not where he was—what that deafening clang, three times sent forth, could mean.

But as his ideas gradually became more clear and collected, all the horrors of his situation and all the details of his dream recurred to his memory.

* * *

Had he really been the object of hell's temptation? Had it indeed been proposed to him to barter his soul for liberty, power, and long life?

He entertained a horrible suspicion—almost amounting to a conviction—that such was the fact; and he thanked Heaven for having provided him with the means to repel the advances of the Tempter.

Then he glanced towards the windows, and averted his eyes with a cold shudder—averted his eyes from the two remaining windows!

He rose from the straw—but his head came in contact with the ceiling, which had now sunk so low, that he could not stand upright in the dungeon!

There, however, upon the little shelf of the door, were the loaf and the pitcher of water, which had been supplied to him while he slept.

"Two windows remaining!" mused Otto to himself, while his heart seemed ready to burst as the images of his wife and children flitted before him. "The bell struck once when the first disappeared—twice when two were gone—and three times when the collapsing walls covered the third! To-morrow it will strike four—and the morning after, five; and then doubtless my doom will be sealed! By whose command do I thus suffer? Who is the enemy that has destined me thus to die? Surely no human being possesses a heart so fiend-like—unless it be indeed the Borgia? Yes—yes; Lucrezia, this is your work:—you seek to punish me for the firmness with which I refused to become the slave of your passions at Rosenthal Castle long ago! Oh! I comprehend it all;—for thou, Lucrezia, art the only living being capable of such atrocity as this! But, if it be the will of Heaven that I die thus, prayers, and not curses, shall mark my last agonising moments!"

It was not, however, without feelings of ineffable horror that Otto surveyed the limited dimensions of that dungeon which now seemed more coffin-like than ever. By whatever strange contrivance it were that those walls were thus made to collapse, and that roof to fall lower, it was impossible to deny that never had infernal cruelty designed a more ingenious method of crushing the spirit by degrees, and the body perhaps in an instant when the time should come.

In the widest part of the iron coffin Otto could now easily touch each side with his extended arms; and at the foot, or lower end, it was so narrow that the door alone at present occupied that space. The fourth night came; and Otto feared to sleep, lest the temptations of hell should be renewed. But he could not walk about—for his head touched the ceiling when he stood upright. He therefore sate upon the straw, and passed the weary, tedious hours in prayer. When, according to the calculation which he made of the lapse of time, light was approaching, he maintained his eyes steadily fixed upon the point where the two remaining windows had stood on the previous day. And soon—by degrees a faint glimmer was perceptible at the head of the iron coffin: then, when the dim ray had somewhat increased in power, the bell suddenly beat—sounding now as if it were just over the hapless prisoner's head, while the iron walls and roof vibrated terrifically with the rebound.

One—two—three—four;—and as the fourth clang fell on Otto's ear, the side against which he was leaning moved noiselessly, but firmly and steadily, inwards. He uttered a loud cry, and flung up his arms in terror;—but his hands encountered the roof, which had now sunk to the level of his head, even as he sate upon the straw.

Instinctively his eyes, a moment averted, were turned again towards the head of the coffin; and the dim light shone upon him through the one remaining window!

"To-morrow—to-morrow!" he cried, clasping his hands together; "and all will be over! Oh! my dear, dear wife—my beloved sons!"

And he wept bitterly.

Those tears relieved him—as much as a man in his awful situation could be relieved; and, perceiving that his food had not been forgotten, he crept along the coffin to the door, now so narrow that a stout person could not have passed through it.

The shelf was still precisely in the middle—for so admirably arranged seemed the fearful mechanism which produced those strange collapses of the coffin's sides and lid, that the precise position of its salient features remained unchanged in reference to each diminished shape.

Firmly impressed with the idea that this was his last day, Otto passed it in the way which the reader, who has studied his character, may conceive; and when night—the fifth night—came, he no longer feared to lie down to rest; for he felt himself nerved to resist all the temptations of hell—were they never so powerful!

Yes—the fifth night had arrived; and Otto Pianalla lay down upon his straw, with the conviction that when the bell should ring in the morning as a signal for the fifth window to disappear, the walls and roof would grasp him in their arms of iron, and enclose him in that coffin of diabolical contrivance.

It was not death that he feared;—but he sorrowed to think that his family was destined to remain in a frightful state of ignorance as to his real fate,—perhaps supported for years and years upon the hope that he might return to them,—until, the heart becoming sick, the very duties of life would seem poisoned, and the end of those whom he loved so devotedly might become painful in the extreme.

In the midst of such reflections as these, he was suddenly startled by a sound—the first save that of the bell and of his own cries which had yet met his ear in the dungeon—emanating from the door.

He listened—listened in the most acute suspense.

Yes; it was indeed a sound as of a trap opening; and immediately afterwards a strong current of air dissipated the almost stifling heat of the iron coffin.

"Otto Pianalla!" said a melodious voice.

Years had passed since the artist had heard those tones;—but he remembered them well—for the voice of Lucrezia Borgia was one of silvery softness.

"Am I indeed, then, the victim of your Highness?" asked Otto. "Oh! is human nature capable of such black ingratitude? Hast thou forgotten, false woman, all I did for thy brother Cæsar?"

"Lucrezia Borgia forgets nothing," was the calm reply; "not even how Otto Pianalla scorned her love in the Castle of Rosenthal. Proud and obdurate man! didst thou not then see me at thy feet—and didst thou not shrink from me as from a viper? Didst thou not even take upon thyself to reproach me for my crimes? But enough of that:—I am not come to reproach—I am here to save thee, if thou wilt."

"Can you ask me if I wish to escape from this horrible prison?" exclaimed Otto, joyfully. "Oh! release me, madam—restore me to my wife and children—let me embrace them once more—and I will pray for thee—I will even speak of thee with gratitude!"

"It is not gratitude that I seek at the hands of Otto Pianalla," answered Lucrezia; "it is love!"

"Oh! would you impose conditions upon me as the price of my release?" cried the artist "Then know, bad woman, that sooner shall these walls crush me to a shapeless mass,—sooner shall this roof fall down this instant on the head which it already touches, even as I speak to thee,—yes—sooner will I die the most horrible of deaths than yield to thy desires!"

"Think not, haughty man," returned Lucrezia, "that your death there will be immediate! Oh no!—that were a mercy too great for those whom the state-vengeance of Ferrara or my own private hatred sends to this living tomb! No!—shouldst thou scorn me now, as thou didst sixteen years ago in the Castle of Rosenthal, prepare thyself for a fate the horrors of which no tongue can describe! For when the fifth sound of to-morrow's bell falls on thine ears, the walls and the roof will move so near each other that they will enclose thee in a space neither a whit larger nor a tittle smaller than thy coffin would be were it duly prepared to receive thy corpse. Therein wilt thou linger for days and days—a prey to starvation—feeding on the flesh of thine hands and arms—and with all the terrific consciousness which can aggravate the hellish torments of thy doom. Otto Pianalla, have I moved thee now?"

"No—no fiend, and not woman, as thou art!" was the

agonising reply. "Avaunt—leave me! I will not yield to thee—go!"

"Then perish in thine obstinacy!" replied Lucrezia; and the trap was immediately closed in the door.

But almost at the same moment the trampling of many feet and the sounds of angry voices fell upon Otto's ears: the bolts and bars of the iron coffin were drawn back— the chains fell with a heavy clank upon the pavement outside—the door was thrown open—lights appeared in the passage—and a loud voice exclaimed, in a commanding tone, "Otto Pianalla, come forth! Thou art free!"

It is beyond the power of language to describe how joyously this invitation was obeyed—how the despair of Otto Pianalla was in a moment changed into the most fervent heart-thrilling delight!

Passing out from the iron coffin, the artist found himself in the presence of an elderly man of noble and imposing aspect, and in whom, by the star that he wore upon his breast, he had no difficulty in recognising the Duke of Ferrara.

The Duchess Lucrezia was a prisoner between two of the ducal guards.

Lucrezia's countenance was ashy pale: but it was evident that she endeavoured as much as possible to conceal her emotions beneath an affectation of haughty indifference.

"Return at once to your family, excellent man," cried the Duke, addressing himself to Pianalla; "but fear not that they have been in sorrow at your absence. Scarcely were you the inmate of this castle, when a message from me relieved them of all anxiety on your account; and an innocent falsehood conveyed to them a reasonable excuse for your separation from them for a few days."

"A thousand thanks, my lord, for this kind consideration on your part!" cried Otto, overjoyed at intelligence so welcome.

"And pardon me," continued the Duke, taking the artist's hand, "if I have allowed you to languish thus long in such horrible suspense as you must have endured. But I required confirmation of that profligacy which I had long suspected—a profligacy on the part of a woman whom, in spite of the ill report of her early life, I raised to be a partner of my ducal throne. Yes, Lucrezia—what have become of all the pledges of fidelity which you made me, when—dazzled by your beauty, overlooking your former errors, and willing to believe your representations that report had exaggerated your failings into enormous crimes —I led you to the altar? But know, vile woman, that you have been betrayed by your own bad agent—your own confidant; and that those words which you ere now uttered to this high-minded man, who nobly refused to purchase life with dishonour, have at length confirmed my long-existing suspicions!"

* * *

"Messer Pianalla, I have naught more to say to you," observed the Duke; "unless it be that I have placed at your disposal a vessel to convey yourself and family to any port whither it may suit your purposes to repair. Farewell—and forget what you have seen or endured within these walls!"

"Your Highness will pardon me," said Otto, glancing towards Lucrezia, "if I venture to implore your mercy in favour of one who—wicked and depraved though she be—"

"Messer Pianalla," interrupted the Duke, sternly, "seek not to place thyself between me and the execution of my sovereign justice. Again I bid thee farewell!"

But Otto still lingered—for, much as he had suffered at the hands of Lucrezia Borgia, he revolted from the idea of the punishment which he feared was in store for her. The Duke perceived his hesitation; and, stamping his foot with rage, cried, "Dost hear? Begone!"

The guards seized upon the artist, and conducted him through the long passages and windings that led to the gate of the Castle of Solitude.

A few minutes after he had thus been removed from the presence of the Duke, the iron coffin received another victim!

Unmoved by her prayers and entreaties—inexorable against her tears and supplications—for the haughty Lucrezia was humbled to the dust when the fiat of her husband went forth—the Duke remained upon the spot while the guards thrust the screaming, wretched, despairing woman into the horrible prison.

Yes—and with the true malignity of the dark Italian vengeance of that age, the Duke quitted not the entrance to the iron coffin throughout the night! And when the first beam of the sun appeared above the eastern hills and grove-topped heights of Lissa, the fearful machinery was set in motion.

Clang—clang went the deafening bell upon the dungeon roof:—five times it struck—while appalling shrieks came from within the living tomb.

And while the echoes of the fifth stroke were yet reverberating through the gloomy passages of the Castle of Solitude, the mysterious engine of death began its dreadful work.

On—on went the closing sides: down—down came the ponderous roof—the fatal machinery no longer moving noiselessly, but collapsing with a hideous crash—yet not so loud as to stifle the agonising screams and shrieks that echoed from the inmate of the iron coffin!

THE MOTHER
AND THE DEAD CHILD

A MOTHER SAT BY HER LITTLE CHILD: she was very sorrowful, and feared that it would die. Its little face was pale, and its eyes were closed. The child drew its breath with difficulty, and sometimes so deeply as if it were sighing; and then the mother looked more sorrowfully than before on the little creature.

Then there was a knock at the door, and a poor old man came in, wrapped up in something that looked like a great horse-cloth, for that keeps warm; and he required it, for it was cold winter. Without, everything was covered with ice and snow, and the wind blew so sharply that it cut one's face.

And as the old man trembled with cold, and the child was quiet for a moment, the mother went and put some beer on the stove in a little pot, to warm it for him. The old man sat down and rocked the cradle, and the mother seated herself on an old chair by him, looked at her sick child that drew its breath so painfully, and seized the little hand.

"You think I shall keep it, do you not?" she asked. "The good God will not take it from me!"

And the old man—he was Death—nodded in such a strange way, that it might just as well mean yes as no. And the mother cast down her eyes, and tears rolled down her cheeks. Her head became heavy: for three days and three nights she had not closed her eyes; and now she slept, but only for a minute; then she started up and shivered with cold.

"What is that?" she asked, and looked round on all sides; but the old man was gone, and her little child was gone; he had taken it with him. And there in the corner the old clock was humming and whirring; the heavy leaden weight ran down to the floor—plump!—and the clock stopped.

But the poor mother rushed out of the house crying for her child.

Out in the snow sat a woman in long black garments, and she said, "Death has been with you in your room; I saw him hasten away with your child: he strides faster than the wind, and never brings back what he has taken away."

"Only tell me which way he has gone," said the mother. "Tell me the way, and I will find him."

"I know him," said the woman in the black garments; "but before I tell you, you must sing me all the songs that you have sung to your child. I love those songs; I have heard them before. I am Night, and I saw your tears when you sang them."

"I will sing them all, all!" said the mother. "But do not detain me, that I may overtake him, and find my child."

But Night sat dumb and still. Then the mother wrung her hands, and sang and wept. And there were many songs, but yet more tears, and then Night said, "Go to the right into the dark fir wood; for I saw Death take that path with your little child."

Deep in the forest there was a cross road, and she did not know which way to take. There stood a blackthorn bush, with not a leaf nor a blossom upon it; for it was in the cold winter-time, and icicles hung from the twigs.

"Have you not seen Death go by, with my little child?"

"Yes," replied the Bush; "but I shall not tell you which way he went unless you warm me on your bosom. I'm freezing to death here, I'm turning to ice."

And she pressed the Blackthorn Bush to her bosom, quite close, that it might be well warmed. And the thorns pierced into her flesh, and her blood oozed out in great drops. But the Blackthorn shot out fresh green leaves, and blossomed in the dark winter night: so warm is the heart of a sorrowing mother! And the Blackthorn Bush told her the way that she should go.

Then she came to a great Lake, on which there was neither ships nor boat. The Lake was not frozen enough to carry her, nor sufficiently open to allow her to wade through, and yet she must cross it if she was to find her child. Then she laid herself down to drink the Lake; and that was impossible for any one to do. But the sorrowing mother thought that perhaps a miracle might be wrought.

"No, that can never succeed," said the Lake. "Let us rather see how we can agree. I'm fond of collecting pearls, and your eyes are the two clearest I have ever seen: if you will weep them out into me I will carry you over into the great greenhouse, where Death lives and cultivates flowers and trees; each of these is a human life."

"Oh, what would I not give to get my child!" said the afflicted mother; and she wept yet more, and her eyes fell into the depths of the Lake, and became two costly pearls. But the Lake lifted her up, as if she sat in a swing, and she was wafted to the opposite shore, where stood a wonderful house, miles in length. One could not tell if it was a mountain containing forests and caves, or a place that had been built. But the poor mother could not see it, for she had wept her eyes out.

"Where shall I find Death, who went away with my little child?" she asked.

"He has not arrived here yet," said an old grey-haired woman, who was going about and watching the hot-house of Death. "How have you found your way here, and who helped you?"

"The good God has helped me," she replied. "He is

merciful, and you will be merciful too. Where—where shall I find my little child?"

"I do not know it," said the old woman, "and you cannot see. Many flowers and trees have faded this night, and Death will soon come and transplant them. You know very well that every human being has his tree of life, or his flower of life, just as each is arranged. They look like other plants, but their hearts beat. Children's hearts can beat too. Think of this. Perhaps you may recognise the beating of your child's heart. But what will you give me if I tell you what more you must do?"

"I have nothing more to give," said the afflicted mother. "But I will go for you to the ends of the earth."

"I have nothing for you to do there," said the old woman. "But you can give me your long black hair. You must know yourself that it is beautiful, and it pleases me. You can take my white hair for it, and that is always something."

"Do you ask for nothing more?" asked she. "I will give you that gladly." And she gave her beautiful hair, and received in exchange the old woman's white hair.

And then they went into the great hot-house of Death, where flowers and trees were growing marvellously intertwined. There stood the fine hyacinths under glass bells, some quite fresh, others somewhat sickly; water-snakes were twining about them, and black crabs clung tightly to the stalks. There stood gallant palm trees, oaks, and

39

plantains, and parsley and blooming thyme. Each tree and flower had its name; each was a human life: the people were still alive, one in China, another in Greenland, scattered about in the world. There were great trees thrust into little pots, so that they stood quite crowded, and were nearly bursting the pots; there was also many a little weakly flower in rich earth, with moss round about it, cared for and tended. But the sorrowful mother bent down over all the smallest plants, and heard the human heart beating in each, and out of millions she recognised that of her child.

"That is it!" she cried, and stretched out her hands over a little crocus flower, which hung down quite sick and pale.

"Do not touch the flower," said the old dame; "but place yourself here; and when Death comes—I expect him every minute—then don't let him pull up the plant, but threaten him that you will do the same to the other plants; then he'll be frightened. He has to account for them all; not one may be pulled up till he receives commission from Heaven."

And all at once there was an icy cold rush through the hall, and the blind mother felt that Death was arriving.

"How did you find your way hither?" said he. "How have you been able to come quicker than I?"

"I am a mother," she answered.

And Death stretched out his long hands towards the little delicate flower; but she kept her hands tight about it, and held it fast; and yet she was full of anxious care lest he should touch one of the leaves. Then Death breathed upon her hands, and she felt that his breath was colder than the icy wind; and her hands sank down powerless.

"You can do nothing against me," said Death.

"But the merciful God can," she replied.

"I only do what He commands," said Death. "I am His gardener. I take all His trees and flowers, and transplant them into the great Paradise gardens, in the unknown land. But how they will flourish there, and how it is there, I may not tell you."

"Give me back my child," said the mother; and she implored and wept. All at once she grasped two pretty flowers with her two hands, and called to Death, "I'll tear off all your flowers, for I am in despair."

"Do not touch them," said Death. "You say you are so unhappy, and now you would make another mother just as unhappy!"

"Another mother?" said the poor woman; and she let the flowers go.

"There are your eyes for you," said Death. "I have fished them out of the lake; they gleamed up quite brightly. I did not know that they were yours. Take them back—they are clearer now than before—and then look down into the deep well close by. I will tell you the names of the two flowers you wanted to pull up, and you will see what you were about to frustrate and destroy."

And she looked down into the well, and it was a happiness to see how one of them became a blessing to the world, how much joy and gladness she diffused around her. And the woman looked at the life of the other, and it was made up of care and poverty, misery and woe.

"Both are the will of God," said Death.

"Which of them is the flower of misfortune, and which the blessed one?" she asked.

"That I may not tell you," answered Death, "but this much you shall hear, that one of these two flowers is that of your child. It was the fate of your child that you saw—the future of your own child."

Then the mother screamed aloud for terror.

"Which of them belongs to my child? Tell me that! Release the innocent child! Let my child free from all that misery! Rather carry it away! Carry it into God's Kingdom! Forget my tears, forget my entreaties, and all that I have done!"

"I do not understand you," said Death. "Will you have your child back, or shall I carry it to that place that you know not?"

Then the mother wrung her hands, and fell on her knees, and prayed to the good God.

"Hear me not when I pray against Thy will, which is at all times the best! Hear me not! hear me not!" And she let her head sink down on her bosom.

And Death went away with her child into the unknown land.

TREGEAGLE

W HO HAS NOT HEARD of the wild spirit Tregeagle? He haunts equally the moor, the rocky coasts, and the blown sand-hills of Cornwall. From north to south, from east to west, this doomed spirit is heard of, and to the day of judgment he is doomed to wander, pursued by avenging fiends. For ever endeavouring to perform some task by which he hopes to secure repose, and being forever defeated. Who has not heard the howling of Tregeagle? When the storms come with all their strength from the Atlantic, and urge themselves upon the rocks around the Land's End, the howls of the spirit are louder than the roaring of the winds. When calms rest upon the ocean, and the waves can scarcely form upon the resting waters, low wailings creep along the coast. These are the wailings of this wandering soul. When midnight is on the moor, or on the mountains, and the night winds whistle amidst the rugged cairns, the shrieks of Tregeagle are distinctly heard. We know then that he is pursued by the demon dogs, and that till daybreak he must fly with all speed before them. The voice of Tregeagle is everywhere, and yet he is unseen by human eye. Every reader wilt at once perceive that Tregeagle belongs to the mythologies of the oldest nations, and that the traditions of this wandering spirit in Cornwall, which centre upon one tyrannical magistrate, are but the appropriation of stories which belong to every age and country. Tradition thus tells Tregeagle's tale.

There are some men who appear to be from their births given over to the will of tormenting demons. Such a man was Tregeagle. He is as old as the hills, yet there are many circumstances in the story of his life which *appear* to remove him from this remote antiquity. Modern legends assert him to belong to comparatively modern times, and say that, without doubt, he was one of the Tregeagles who once owned Trevorder near Bodmin. We have not, however, much occasion to trouble ourselves with the man or his life; it is with the death and the subsequent existence of a myth that we are concerned.

Certain it is that the man Tregeagle was diabolically wicked. He seems to have been urged on from one crime to another until the cup of sin was overflowing.

Tregeagle was wealthy beyond most men of his time, and his wealth purchased for him that immunity which the Church, in her degenerate days, too often accorded to those who could aid, with their gold or power, the sensual

priesthood. As a magistrate, he was tyrannical and unjust, and many an innocent man was wantonly sacrificed by him for the purpose of hiding his own dark deeds. As a landlord, he was rapacious and unscrupulous, and frequently so involved his tenants in his toils, that they could not escape his grasp. The stain of secret murder clings to his memory, and he is said to have sacrificed a sister whose goodness stood between him and his demon passions; his wife and children perished victims to his cruelties. At length death drew near to relieve the land of a monster whose name was a terror to all who heard it. Devils waited to secure the soul they had won, and Tregeagle in terror gave to the priesthood wealth, that they might fight with them and save his soul from eternal fire. Desperate was the struggle, but the powerful exorcisms of the banded brotherhood of a neighbouring monastery drove back the evil ones, and Tregeagle slept with his fathers, safe in the custody of the churchmen, who buried him with high honours in St Breock Church. They sang chants and read prayers above his grave, to secure the soul which they thought they had saved. But Tregeagle was not fated to rest. Satan desired still to gain possession of such a gigantic sinner, and we can only refer what ensued to the influence of the wicked spiritings of his ministers.

A dispute arose between two wealthy families respecting the ownership of extensive lands around Bodmin. The question had been rendered more difficult by the nefarious conduct of Tregeagle, who had acted as steward to one of the claimants, and who had destroyed ancient deeds, forged others, and indeed made it appear that he was the real proprietor of the domain. Large portions of the land Tregeagle had sold, and other parts were leased upon long terms, he having received all the money and appropriated it. His death led to inquiries, and then the transactions were gradually brought to light. Involving, as this did, large sums of money—and indeed it was a question upon which turned the future well-doing or ruin of a family—it was fought by the lawyers with great pertinacity. The legal questions had been argued several times before the judges at the assizes. The trials had been deferred, new trials had been sought for and granted, and every possible plan known to the lawyers for postponing the settlement of a suit had been tried. A day was at length fixed, upon which a final decision must be come to, and a special jury was sworn to administer justice between the contending parties. Witnesses innumerable were examined as to the validity of a certain deed, and the balance of evidence was equally suspended. The judge was about to sum up the case and refer the question to the jury, when the defendant in the case, coming into court, proclaimed aloud that he had yet another witness to produce. There was a strange silence in the judgment hall. It was felt that something chilling to the soul was amongst them, and there was a simultaneous throb of terror as Tregeagle was led into the witness-box.

When the awe-struck assembly had recovered, the lawyers for the defendant commenced their examination, which was long and terrible. The result, however, was the disclosure of an involved system of fraud, of which the honest defendant had been the victim, and the jury unhesitatingly gave a verdict in his favour.

The trial over, everyone expected to see the spectre-witness removed. There, however, he stood, powerless to fly, although he evidently desired to do so. Spirits of darkness were waiting to bear him away, but some spell of holiness prevented them from touching him. There was a struggle with the good and the evil angels for this sinner's soul, and the assembled court appeared frozen with horror. At length the judge with dignity commanded the defendant to remove his witness.

"To bring him from the grave has been to me so dreadful a task, that I leave him to your care, and that of the Priors, by whom he was so beloved." Having said this, the defendant left the court.

The churchmen were called in, and long were the deliberations between them and the lawyers as to the best mode of disposing of Tregeagle.

They could resign him to the devil at once, but by long trial the worst of crimes might be absolved, and as good churchmen they could not sacrifice a human soul. The only thing was to give the spirit some task, difficult beyond the power of human nature, which might be extended far into eternity. Time might thus gradually soften the obdurate soul, which still retained all the black dyes of the sins done in the flesh, that by infinitely slow degrees repentance might exert its softening power. The spell therefore put upon Tregeagle was, that as long as he was employed on some endless assigned task, there should be hope of salvation, and that he should be secure from the assaults of the devil as long as he laboured steadily. A moment's rest was fatal; labour unresting, and for ever, was his doom.

One of the lawyers, remembering that Dosmery Pool was bottomless, and that a thorn-bush which had been flung into it, but a few weeks before, had made its appearance in Falmouth Harbour, proposed that Tregeagle might be employed to empty this profound lake. Then one of the churchmen, to make the task yet more enduring, proposed that it should be performed by the aid of a limpet-shell having a hole in it.

This was agreed to, and the required incantations were duly made. Bound by mystical spells, Tregeagle was removed to the dark moors, and duly set to work. Year after year passed by, and there, day and night, summer and winter, storm and shine, Tregeagle was bending over the dark water, working hard with his perforated shell; yet the pool remained at the same level.

His old enemy the devil kept a careful eye on the doomed one, resolving, if possible, to secure so choice an example of evil. Often did he raise tempests sufficiently wild, as he supposed, to drive Tregeagle from his work, knowing that if he failed for a season to labour, he could seize and secure him. These were long tried in vain; but at length an auspicious hour presented itself.

Nature was at war with herself, the elements had lost their balance, and there was a terrific struggle to recover it. Lightnings flashed and coiled like fiery snakes around the rocks of Roughtor. Fire-balls fell on the desert moors and hissed in the accursed lake. Thunders peeled through the heavens, and echoed from hill to hill; an earthquake shook the solid earth, and terror was on all living. The winds arose and raged with a fury which was irresistible, and hail beat so mercilessly on all things that it spread death around. Long did Tregeagle stand the "pelting of the pitiless storm," but at length he yielded to its force and fled. The demons in crowds were at his heels. He doubled, however, on his pursuers, and returned to the lake; but so rapid were they that he could not rest the required moment to dip his shell in the now seething waters.

Three times he fled round the lake, and the evil ones pursued him. Then, feeling that there was no safety for him near Dosmery Pool, he sprang swifter than the wind across it, shrieking with agony, and thus—since the devils cannot cross water, and were obliged to go round the lake—he gained on them and fled over the moor.

Away, away went Tregeagle, faster and faster the dark spirits pursuing, and they had nearly overtaken him, when he saw Roach Rock and its chapel before him. He rushed up the rocks, with giant power clambered to the eastern window, and dashed his head through it, thus securing the shelter of its sanctity. The defeated demons retired, and long and loud were their wild wailings in the air. The inhabitants of the moors and of the neighbouring towns slept not a wink that night.

Tregeagle was safe, his head was within the holy church, though his body was exposed on a bare rock to the storm. Earnest were the prayers of the blessed hermit in his cell on the rock, to be relieved from his nocturnal and sinful visitor.

In vain were the recluse's prayers. Day after day, as he knelt at the altar, the ghastly head of the doomed sinner grinned horridly down upon him. Every holy ejaculation fell upon Tregeagle's ear like molten iron. He writhed and shrieked under the torture; but legions of devils filled the air, ready to seize him, if for a moment he withdrew his head from the sanctuary. Sabbath after Sabbath the little chapel on the rock was rendered a scene of sad confusion by the interruptions which Tregeagle caused. Men trembled with fear at his agonising cries, and women swooned. At length the place was deserted, and even the saint of the rock was wasting to death by the constant perturbation in which he was kept by the unholy spirit, and the demons who, like carrion birds, swarmed around the holy cairn. Things could not go on thus. The monks of Bodmin and the priests from the neighbouring churches gathered together, and the result of their long and anxious deliberations was that Tregeagle, guarded by two saints, should be taken to the north coast, near Padstow, and employed in making trusses of sand, and ropes of sand with which to bind them. By powerful spell, Tregeagle was removed from Roach, and fixed upon the sandy snores of the Padstow district. Sinners are seldom permitted to enjoy any peace of soul. As the ball of sand grew into form, the tides rose, and the breakers spread out the sands again a level sheet; again was it packed together and again washed away. Toil! toil! toil! day and night unrestingly, sand on sand grew with each hour, and ruthlessly the ball was swept, by one blow of a sea wave, along the shore.

The cries of Tregeagle were dreadful; and as the destruction of the sand heap was constantly recurring, a constantly increasing despair gained the mastery over hope, and the ravings of the baffled soul were louder than the roarings of the winter tempest.

Baffled in making trusses of sand, Tregeagle seized upon the loose particles and began to spin them into a rope. Long and patiently did he pursue his task, and hope once more rose like a star out of the midnight darkness of despair. A rope was forming, when a storm came up with all its fury from the Atlantic, and swept the particles of sand away over the hills.

The inhabitants of Padstow had seldom any rest. At every tide the howlings of Tregeagle banished sleep from each eye. But now so fearful were the sounds of the doomed soul, in the madness of the struggle between hope and despair, that the people fled the town, and clustered upon the neighbouring plains, praying, as with one voice, to be relieved from the sad presence of this monster.

St. Petroc, moved by the tears and petitions of the people, resolved to remove the spirit; and by the intense earnestness of his prayers, after long wrestling, he subdued Tregeagle to his will. Having chained him with the bonds which the saint had forged with his own hands, every link of which had been welded with a prayer, St. Petroc led the spirit away from the north coast, and stealthily placed him on the southern shores.

In those days Ella's Town, now Helston, was a flourishing port. Ships sailed into the estuary, up to the town, and they brought all sorts of merchandise, and returned with cargoes of tin from the mines of Breage and Wendron.

The wily monk placed his charge at Bareppa, and there condemned him to carry sacks of sand across the estuary of the Loo, and to empty them at Porthleven, until the beach was clean down to the rocks. The priest was a good observer. He knew that the sweep of the tide was from Trewavas Head round the coast towards the Lizard, and that the sand would be carried back steadily and speedily as fast as the spirit could remove it.

Long did Tregeagle labour; and, of course, in vain. His struggles were giant-like to perform his task, but he saw the sands return as regularly as he removed them. The sufferings of the poor fishermen who inhabited the coast around Porthleven were great. As the howlings of Tregeagle disturbed the dwellers in Padstow, so did they now distress those toil-worn men.

"When sorrow is highest
Relief is nighest."

And a mischievous demon-watcher, in pure wantonness, brought that relief to those fishers of the sea.

Tregeagle was laden with a sack of sand of enormous size, and was wading across the mouth of the estuary, when one of those wicked devils, who were kept ever near Tregeagle, in very idleness tripped up the heavily-laden spirit. The sea was raging with the irritation of a passing storm; and as Tregeagle fell, the sack was seized by the waves, and its contents poured out across this arm of the sea.

There, to this day, it rests a bar of sand, fatally destroying the harbour of Ella's Town. The rage of the inhabitants of this seaport—now destroyed—was great; and, with all their priests, away they went to the Loo Bar, and assailed their destroyer. Against human anger Tregeagle was proof. The shock of tongues fell harmlessly on his ear, and the assault of human weapons was unavailing.

By the aid of the priests, and faith-inspired prayers, the bonds were once more placed upon Tregeagle; and he was, by the force of bell, book, and candle, sent to the Land's End. There he would find no harbour to destroy, and but few people to terrify. His task was to sweep the sands from Porthcurnow Cove round the headland called Tol-Peden-Penwith, into Nanjisal Cove. Those who know that rugged headland, with its cubical masses of granite, piled in Titanic grandeur one upon another, will appreciate the task; and when to all the difficulties are added the strong sweep of the Atlantic current—that portion of the Gulf-stream which washes our southern shores—it will be evident that the melancholy spirit has, indeed, a task which must endure until the world shall end.

Even until to-day is Tregeagle labouring at his task. In calms his wailing is heard; and those sounds which some call the "soughing of the wind" are known to be the moanings of Tregeagle; while the coming storms are predicated by the fearful roarings of this condemned mortal.

THE DUTCH
OFFICER'S STORY

"WELL, I THINK NOTHING can be so cowardly as to be afraid to own the truth," said the pretty Madame de B., an English woman who had married a Dutch officer of distinction.

"Are you really venturing to accuse the General of cowardice?" said Madame L.

"Yes," said Madame de B.; "I want him to tell Mrs Crowe a ghost story—a thing that he saw himself—and he pooh, poohs it, though he owned it to me before we were married, and since too, saying that he never could have believed such a thing if he had not seen it himself."

While the wife was making this little tirade, the husband looked as if she was accusing him of picking somebody's pocket *il perdait contenance* quite. "Now, look at him," she said, "don't you see guilt in his face, Mrs Crowe!"

"Decidedly," I answered; "so experienced a seeker of ghost stories as myself cannot fail to recognise the symptoms. I always find that when the circumstances are mere hearsay, and happened to nobody knows who, people are very ready to tell it; when it has happened to one of their own family, they are considerably less communicative, and will only tell it under protest: but when they are themselves the parties concerned it is the most difficult thing imaginable to induce them to relate the thing seriously, and with its details. They say they have forgotten it, and don't believe it; and as an evidence of their incredulity they affect to laugh at the whole affair. If the General will tell me the story I will think it quite as decisive a proof of courage as he ever gave in the field."

Betwixt bantering and persuasion, we succeeded in our object, and the General began as follows:—

"You know the Belgian Rebellion" (he always called it so) "took place in 1830. It broke out at Brussels on the 28th of August, and we immediately advanced with a considerable force to attack that city; but as the Prince of Orange hoped to bring people to reason without bloodshed, we encamped at Vilvorde, whilst he entered Brussels alone to hold a conference with the armed people. I was a Lieutenant-Colonel then, and commanded the 20th Foot, to which regiment I had been lately appointed.

"We had been three or four days in cantonment, when I heard two of the men, who were digging a little drain at the back of my tent, talking of Jokel Falck, a private in my regiment, who was noted for his extraordinary disposition to somnolence. One of them remarked that he would certainly have got into trouble for being asleep on his post the previous night if it had not been for Mungo. 'I don't know how many times he has saved him,' added he.

"To which the other answered that Mungo was a very valuable friend, and had saved many a man from punishment.

"This was the first time I had ever heard of Mungo, and I rather wondered who it was they alluded to; but the conversation slipped from my mind, and I never thought of asking anybody.

"Shortly after this I was going my rounds, being field-officer of the day, when I saw, by the moonlight, the sentry at one of the outposts stretched upon the ground. I was some way off when I first perceived him; and I only knew what the object was from the situation, and because I saw the glitter of his accoutrements; but almost at the same moment that I discovered him, I observed a large, black Newfoundland dog trotting towards him. The man rose as the dog approached, and had got upon his legs before I reached the spot. This occupied the space of about two minutes—perhaps not so much.

"'You were asleep at your post,' I said; and turning to the mounted orderly that attended me, I told him to go back and bring a file of the guard to take him prisoner, and to send a sentry to relieve him.

"'*Non, mon Colonel*,' said he; and from the way he spoke, I perceived he was intoxicated; 'it's all the fault of that *damné* Mungo. *Il m'a manque.*'

"But I paid no attention to what he said, and rode on, concluding Mungo was some slang term of the men for drink.

"Some evenings after this, I was riding back from my brother's quarters—he was in the 15th, and was stationed about a mile from us—when I remarked the same dog I had seen before trot up to a sentry who, with his legs crossed, was leaning against a wall. The man started, and began walking backwards and forwards on his beat. I recognised the dog by a large white streak on his side—all the rest of his coat being black.

"When I came up to the man, I saw it was Jokel Falck, and although I could not have said he was asleep, I strongly suspected that was the fact.

"'You had better take care of yourself, my man,' said I. 'I have half a mind to have you relieved, and make a prisoner of you. I believe I should have found you asleep on your post if that dog had not roused you.'

"Instead of looking penitent, as was usual on these occasions, I saw a half-smile on the man's face as he saluted me.

"'Whose dog is that?' I asked my servant, as I rode away.

"'*Je ne sais pas, mon Colonel*,' he answered, smiling too.

"On the same evening at mess, I heard one of the subalterns say to the officer who sat next him, 'It's a fact, I assure you, and they call him Mungo.'

"'That's a new name they've got for Schnapps, isn't it?' I said.

"'No, sir; it's the name of a dog,' replied the young man, laughing.

"'A black Newfoundland, with a large white streak on his flank?'

"'Yes, sir, I believe that is the description,' replied he, tittering still.

"'I have seen that dog two or three times,' said I. 'I saw him this evening—who does he belong to?'

"'Well, sir, that is a difficult question,' answered the lad; and I heard his companion say—'To Old Nick, I should think.'

"'Do you mean to say you've really seen Mungo?' said somebody at the table.

"'If Mungo is a large Newfoundland—black, with a white streak on its side—I saw him just now. Who does he belong to?'

"By this time the whole mess-table was in a titter, with the exception of one old captain, a man who had been years in the regiment. He was of very humble extraction, and had risen by merit to his present position.

"'I believe Captain T. is better acquainted with Mungo

than anybody present,' answered Major P., with a sneer. 'Perhaps he can tell you who he belongs to.'

"The laughter increased, and I saw there was some joke; but not understanding what it meant, I said to Captain T.—

"'Does the dog belong to Jokel Falck?'

"'No, sir,' he replied; 'the dog belongs to nobody now. He once belonged to an officer called Joseph Atveld.'

"'Belonging to this regiment?'

"'Yes, sir.'

"'He is dead, I suppose?'

"'Yes, sir, he is.'

"'And the dog has attached himself to the regiment?'

"'Yes, sir.'

"During this conversation, the suppressed laughter continued, and every eye was fixed on Captain T., who answered me shortly, but with the utmost gravity.

"'In short,' said the Major, contemptuously, 'according to Captain T., Mungo is the ghost of a deceased dog.'

"This announcement was received with shouts of laughter, in which, I confess, I joined, whilst Captain T. still maintained an unmoved gravity.

"'It is easier to laugh at such a thing than to believe it, sir,' said he. 'I believe it, because I know it.'

"I smiled, and turned the conversation.

"If anybody at the table except Captain T. had made such an assertion as this, I should have ridiculed them without mercy; but he was an old man, and from the circumstances I have mentioned regarding his origin, we were careful not to offend him; so no more was said about Mungo, and in the hurry of events that followed, I never thought of it again. We marched on to Brussels the next day; and after that, had enough to do till we went to Antwerp, where we were besieged by the French the following year.

"During the siege, I sometimes heard the name of Mungo again; and, one night, when I was visiting the guards and sentries as grand rounds, I caught a glimpse of him, and I felt sure that the man he was approaching when I observed him had been asleep; but he was screened by an angle of the bastion, and by the time I turned the corner, he was moving about.

"This brought to my mind all I had heard about the dog; and as the circumstance was curious, in any point of view, I mentioned what I had seen to Captain T. the next day, saying—

"'I saw your friend Mungo, last night!'

"'Did you, sir?' said he. 'It's a strange thing! No doubt, the man was asleep!'

"'But do you seriously mean to say that you believe this to be a visionary dog, and not a dog of flesh and blood?'

"'I do, sir. I have been quizzed enough about it; and, once or twice, have nearly got into a quarrel, because people will persist in laughing at what they know nothing about;

but as sure as that is a sword you hold in your hand, so sure is that dog a spectre, or ghost—if such a word is applicable to a four-footed beast!'

"'But, it's impossible!' I said. 'What reason have you for such an extraordinary belief?'

"'Why, you know, sir, man and boy, I have been in the regiment all my life. I was born in it. My father was pay-sergeant of No. 3 Company when he died; and I have seen Mungo myself, perhaps twenty times, and known, positively, of others seeing him twice as many more.'

"'Very possibly; but that is no proof that it is not some dog that has attached himself to the regiment.'

"'But I have seen and heard of the dog for fifty years, sir; and my father before me had seen and heard of him as long!'

"'Well, certainly, that is extraordinary—if you are sure of it, and that it's the same dog!'

"'It's a remarkable dog, sir. You won't see another like it with that large white streak on his flank. He won't let one of our sentries be found asleep if he can help it; unless, indeed, the fellow is drunk. He seems to have less care of drunkards, but Mungo has saved many a man from punishment. I was once not a little indebted to him myself. My sister was married out of the regiment, and we had had a bit of a festivity, and drank rather too freely at the wedding, so that when I mounted guard that night—I wasn't to say drunk, but my head was a little gone, or so, and I should have been caught nodding, but Mungo, knowing, I suppose, that I was not an habitual drunkard, woke me just in time.'

"'How did he wake you?' I asked.

"'I was roused by a short, sharp bark, that sounded close to my ears. I started, and had just time to catch a glimpse of Mungo before he vanished!'

"'Is that the way he always wakes the men?'

"'So they say; and as they wake, he disappears.'

"I recollected now, that on each occasion when I had observed the dog, I had, somehow, lost sight of him in an instant; and, my curiosity being awakened, I asked Captain T. if ours were the only men he took charge of, or whether he showed the same attention to those of other regiments.

"'Only the 20th, sir; the tradition is, that after the battle of Fontenoy, a large black mastiff was found lying beside a dead officer. Although he had a dreadful wound from a sabre-cut on his flank, and was much exhausted from loss of blood, he would not leave the body; and even after we buried it, he could not be enticed from the spot.

"'The men, interested by the fidelity and attachment of the animal, bound up his wounds, and fed and tended him; and he became the dog of the regiment. It is said that they had taught him to go his rounds before the guards and sentries were visited, and to wake any men that slept. How this may be, I cannot say; but he remained with the regiment till his death, and was buried with all the respect they could show him. Since that he has shown his gratitude in the way I tell you, and of which you have seen some instances.'

"'I suppose the white streak is the mark of the sabre-cut. I wonder you never fired at him.'

"'God forbid, sir, I should do such a thing,' said Captain T., looking sharp round at me. 'It's said that a man did so once, and that he never had any luck afterwards; that may be a superstition, but I confess I wouldn't take a good deal to do it.'

"'If, as you believe, it's a spectre, it could not be hurt, you know; I imagine ghostly dogs are impervious to bullets.'

"'No doubt, sir; but I shouldn't like to try the experiment. Besides, it would be useless, as I am convinced already.'

"I pondered a good deal upon this conversation with the old captain. I had never for a moment entertained the idea that such a thing was possible. I should have as much expected to meet the Minotaur or a flying dragon as a ghost of any sort, especially the ghost of a dog; but the evidence here was certainly startling. I had never observed anything like weakness and credulity about T.; moreover, he was a man of known courage, and very much respected in the regiment. In short, so much had his earnestness on the subject staggered me, that I resolved, whenever it was my turn to visit the guards and sentries, that I would carry a pistol with me ready primed and loaded, in order to settle the question. If T. was right there would be an interesting fact established, and no harm done; if, as I could not help suspecting, it was a cunning trick of the men, who had trained this dog to wake them, while they kept up the farce of the spectre, the animal would be well out of the way; since their reliance on him no doubt led them to give way to drowsiness when they would otherwise have struggled against it; indeed, though none of our men had been detected—thanks, perhaps, to Mungo—there had been so much negligence lately in the garrison that the General had issued very severe orders on the subject.

"However, I carried my pistol in vain; I did not happen to fall in with Mungo; and some time afterwards, on hearing the thing alluded to at the mess-table, I mentioned what I had done, adding, 'Mungo is too knowing, I fancy, to run the risk of getting a bullet in him.'

"'Well,' said Major R., 'I should like to have a shot at him, I confess. If I thought I had any chance of seeing him, I'd certainly try it; but I've never seen him at all.'

"'Your best chance,' said another, 'is when Jokel Falck is on duty. He is such a sleepy scoundrel, that the men say if it was not for Mungo he'd pass half his time in the guard house.'

"'If I could catch him, I'd put an ounce of lead into him; that he may rely on.'

"'Into Jokel Falck, sir,' said one of the subs, laughing.

"'No, sir,' replied Major R.; 'into Mungo—and I'll do it too.'

"'Better not, sir,' said Captain T., gravely, provoking thereby a general titter round the table.

"Shortly after this, as I was one night going to my quarters, I saw a mounted orderly ride in and call out a file of the guard to take a prisoner.

"'What's the matter?' I asked.

"'One of the sentries asleep on his post, sir; I believe it's Jokel Falck.'

"It will be the last time, whoever it is,' I said; 'for the General is determined to shoot the next man that's caught.'

"'I should have thought Mungo had stood Jokel Falck's friend so often, that he'd never allow him to be caught,' said the adjutant. 'Mungo has neglected his duty.'

"'No, sir,' said the orderly, gravely. 'Mungo would have waked him, but Major R. shot at him.'

"'And killed him?' I said.

"The man made no answer, but touched his cap and rode away.

"I heard no more of the affair that night; but the next morning at a very early hour, my servant woke me, saying that Major R. wished to speak to me. I desired he should be admitted, and the moment he entered the room, I saw by his countenance that something serious had occurred; of course I thought the enemy had gained some unexpected advantage during the night, and sat up in bed, inquiring eagerly what had happened.

"To my surprise, he pulled out his pocket-handkerchief and burst into tears. He had married a native of Antwerp, and his wife was in the city at this time. The first thing that occurred to me was that she had met with some accident, and I mentioned her name.

"'No, no,' he said; 'my son, my boy, my poor Fritz!'

"You know that in our service every officer first enters his regiment as a private soldier, and for a certain space of time does all the duties of that position. The Major's son, Fritz, was thus in his noviciate. I concluded he had been killed by a stray shot, and for a minute or two I remained in this persuasion, the Major's speech being choked by his sobs. The first words he uttered were

"'Would to God I had taken Captain T.'s advice!'

"'About what?' I said. 'What has happened to Fritz?'

"'You know,' said he, 'yesterday I was field officer of the day; and when I was going my rounds last night, I happened to ask my orderly, who was assisting to put on my sash, what men we had told off for the guard. Amongst others, he named Jokel Falck, and remembering the conversation the other day at the mess-table, I took one of my pistols out of the holster, and, after loading it, put it in my pocket. I did not expect to see the dog, for I had never seen him; but as I had no doubt the story of the spectre was some dodge of the men, I determined, if ever I did, to have a shot at him. As I was going through the Place de Meyer, I fell in with the General, who joined me, and we rode on together, talking of the siege. I had forgotten all about the dog, but when we came to the rampart, above the Bastion du Matte, I suddenly saw exactly such an animal as the one described trotting beneath us. I knew there must be a sentry immediately below where we rode, though I could not see him, and I had no doubt that the animal was making towards him; so, without saying a word, I drew out my pistol and fired, at the same moment jumping off my horse, in order to look over the bastion, and get a sight of the man. Without comprehending what I was about, the General did the same, and there we saw the sentry, lying on his face, fast asleep.'

"'And the body of the dog?' said I.

"'Nowhere to be seen,' he answered; 'and yet I must have hit him I fired bang into him. The General says it must have been a delusion, for he was looking exactly in the same direction, and saw no dog at all—but I am certain I saw him, so did the orderly.'

"'But Fritz?' I said.

"'It was Fritz—Fritz was the sentry,' said the Major, with a fresh burst of grief. 'The court-martial sits this morning, and my boy will be shot unless interest can be made with the General to grant him a pardon.'

"I rose and dressed myself immediately, but with little hope of success. Poor Fritz being the son of an officer was against him rather than otherwise—it would have been considered an act of favouritism to spare him. He was shot; his poor mother died of a broken heart, and the Major left the service immediately after the surrender of the city."

"And have you ever seen Mungo again?" said I.

"No," he replied; "but I have heard of others seeing him."

"And are you convinced that it was a spectre, and not a dog of flesh and blood?"

"I fancy I was then—but, of course, one can't believe—"

"Oh no," I rejoined; "oh no; never mind facts if they don't fit into our theories."

THE CASK OF AMONTILLADO

THE THOUSAND INJURIES OF Fortunato I had borne as I best could, but when he ventured upon insult, I vowed revenge. You, who so well knew the nature of my soul, will not suppose, however, that I gave utterance to a threat. At length I would be avenged; this was a point definitively settled—but the very definitiveness with which it was resolved precluded the idea of risk. I must not only punish, but punish with impunity. A wrong is unredressed when retribution overtakes its redresser. It is equally unredressed when the avenger fails to make himself felt as such to him who has done the wrong.

It must be understood that neither by word nor deed had I given Fortunato cause to doubt my good will. I continued, as was my wont, to smile in his face, and he did not perceive that my smile now was at the thought of his immolation.

He had a weak point—this Fortunato—although in other regards he was a man to be respected and even feared.

He prided himself on his connoisseurship in wine. Few Italians have the true virtuoso spirit. For the most part their enthusiasm is adopted to suit the time and opportunity to practise imposture upon the British and Austrian millionaires. In painting and gemmary, Fortunato, like his countrymen, was a quack, but in the matter of old wines he was sincere. In this respect I did not differ from him materially; I was skilful in the Italian vintages myself, and bought largely whenever I could.

It was about dusk, one evening during the supreme madness of the carnival season, that I encountered my friend. He accosted me with excessive warmth, for he had been drinking much. The man wore motley. He had on a tight-fitting parti-striped dress, and his head was surmounted by the conical cap and bells. I was so pleased to see him that I thought I should never have done wringing his hand.

I said to him—"My dear Fortunato, you are luckily met. How remarkably well you are looking to-day! But I have received a pipe of what passes for Amontillado, and I have my doubts."

"How?" said he, "Amontillado? A pipe? Impossible? And in the middle of the carnival?"

"I have my doubts," I replied; "and I was silly enough to pay the full Amontillado price without consulting you in the matter. You were not to be found, and I was fearful of losing a bargain."

"Amontillado!"

"I have my doubts."

"Amontillado!"

"And I must satisfy them."

"Amontillado!"

"As you are engaged, I am on my way to Luchesi. If any one has a critical turn, it is he. He will tell me—"

"Luchesi cannot tell Amontillado from Sherry."

"And yet some fools will have it that his taste is a match for your own."

"Come, let us go."

"Whither?"

"To your vaults."

"My friend, no; I will not impose upon your good nature. I perceive you have an engagement. Luchesi—"

"I have no engagement; come."

"My friend, no. It is not the engagement, but the severe cold with which I perceive you are afflicted. The vaults are insufferably damp. They are encrusted with nitre."

"Let us go, nevertheless. The cold is merely nothing. Amontillado! You have been imposed upon; and as for Luchesi, he cannot distinguish Sherry from Amontillado."

Thus speaking, Fortunato possessed himself of my arm. Putting on a mask of black silk, and drawing a *roquelaure* closely about my person, I suffered him to hurry me to my palazzo.

There were no attendants at home; they had absconded to make merry in honour of the time. I had told them that I should not return until the morning, and had given them explicit orders not to stir from the house. These orders were sufficient, I well knew, to insure their immediate disappearance, one and all, as soon as my back was turned.

I took from their sconces two flambeaux, and giving one to Fortunato, bowed him through several suites of rooms to the archway that led into the vaults. I passed down a long and winding staircase, requesting him to be cautious as he followed. We came at length to the foot of the descent, and stood together on the damp ground of the catacombs of the Montresors.

The gait of my friend was unsteady, and the bells upon his cap jingled as he strode.

"The pipe," said he.

"It is farther on," said I; "but observe the white web-work which gleams from these cavern walls."

He turned towards me, and looked into my eyes with two filmy orbs that distilled the rheum of intoxication.

"Nitre?" he asked, at length.

"Nitre," I replied. "How long have you had that cough?"

"Ugh! ugh! ugh!—ugh! ugh! ugh!—ugh! ugh! ugh!—ugh! ugh! ugh!—ugh! ugh! ugh!"

My poor friend found it impossible to reply for many minutes.

"It is nothing," he said, at last.

"Come," I said, with decision, "we will go back; your health is precious. You are rich, respected, admired, beloved; you are happy, as once I was. You are a man to be missed. For me it is no matter. We will go back; you will be ill, and I cannot be responsible. Besides, there is Luchesi—"

"Enough," he said; "the cough is a mere nothing; it will not kill me. I shall not die of a cough."

"True—true," I replied; "and, indeed, I had no intention of alarming you unnecessarily, but you should use all proper caution. A draught of this Médoc will defend us from the damps."

Here I knocked off the neck of a bottle which I drew from a long row of its fellows that lay upon the mould.

"Drink," I said, presenting him the wine.

He raised it to his lips with a leer. He paused and nodded to me familiarly while his bells jingled.

"I drink," he said, "to the buried that repose around us."

"And I to your long life."

He again took my arm, and we proceeded.

"These vaults," he said, "are extensive."

"The Montresors," I replied, "were a great and numerous family."

"I forget your arms."

"A huge human foot *d'or*, in a field *azure*; the foot

crushes a serpent *rampant* whose fangs are imbedded in the heel."

"And the motto?"

"Nemo me impune lacessit."

"Good!" he said.

The wine sparkled in his eyes and the bells jingled. My own fancy grew warm with the Médoc. We had passed through walls of piled bones, with casks and puncheons intermingling, into the inmost recesses of the catacombs. I paused again, and this time I made bold to seize Fortunato by an arm above the elbow.

"The nitre!" I said: "see, it increases. It hangs like moss upon the vaults. We are below the river's bed. The drops of moisture trickle among the bones. Come, we will go back ere it is too late. Your cough—"

"It is nothing," he said; "let us go on. But first, another draught of the Médoc."

I broke and reached him a flacon of De Grave. He emptied it at a breath. His eyes flashed with a fierce light. He laughed and threw the bottle upwards with a gesticulation I did not understand. I looked at him in surprise. He repeated the movement—a grotesque one.

"You do not comprehend?" he said.

"Not I," I replied.

"Then you are not of the brotherhood."

"How?"

"You are not of the masons."

"Yes, yes," I said, "yes, yes."

"You? Impossible! A mason?"

"A mason," I replied.

"A sign," he said.

"It is this," I answered, producing a trowel from beneath the folds of my *roquelaure*.

"You jest," he exclaimed, recoiling a few paces. "But let us proceed to the Amontillado."

"Be it so," I said, replacing the tool beneath the cloak, and again offering him my arm. He leaned upon it heavily. We continued our route in search of the Amontillado. We passed through a range of low arches, descended, passed on, and descending again, arrived at a deep crypt, in which the foulness of the air caused our flambeaux rather to glow than flame.

At the most remote end of the crypt there appeared another less spacious. Its walls had been lined with human remains piled to the vault overhead, in the fashion of the great catacombs of Paris. Three sides of this interior crypt were still ornamented in this manner. From the fourth the bones had been thrown down, and lay promiscuously upon the earth, forming at one point a mound of some size. Within the wall thus exposed by the displacing of the bones, we perceived a still interior recess, in depth about four feet, in width three, in height six or seven.

It seemed to have been constructed for no special use within itself, but formed merely the interval between two of the colossal supports of the roof of the catacombs, and was backed by one of their circumscribing walls of solid granite.

It was in vain that Fortunato, uplifting his dull torch, endeavoured to pry into the depths of the recess. Its termination the feeble light did not enable us to see.

"Proceed," I said; "herein is the Amontillado. As for Luchesi—"

"He is an ignoramus," interrupted my friend, as he stepped unsteadily forward, while I followed immediately at his heels. In an instant he had reached the extremity of the niche, and finding his progress arrested by the rock, stood stupidly bewildered. A moment more and I had fettered him to the granite. In its surface were two iron staples, distant from each other about two feet, horizontally. From one of these depended a short chain, from the other a padlock. Throwing the links about his waist, it was but the work of a few seconds to secure it. He was too much astounded to resist. Withdrawing the key I stepped back from the recess.

"Pass your hand," I said, "over the wall; you cannot help feeling the nitre. Indeed it is very damp. Once more let me implore you to return. No? Then I must positively leave you. But I must first render you all the little attentions in my power."

"The Amontillado!" ejaculated my friend, not yet recovered from his astonishment.

"True," I replied; "the Amontillado."

As I said these words I busied myself among the pile of bones of which I have before spoken. Throwing them aside, I soon uncovered a quantity of building stone and mortar. With these materials and with the aid of my trowel, I began vigorously to wall up the entrance of the niche.

I had scarcely laid the first tier of the masonry when I discovered that the intoxication of Fortunato had in a great measure worn off. The earliest indication I had of this was a low moaning cry from the depth of the recess. It was not the cry of a drunken man. There was then a long and obstinate silence. I laid the second tier, and the third, and the fourth; and then I heard the furious vibrations of the chain. The noise lasted for several minutes, during which, that I might hearken to it with the more satisfaction, I ceased my labours and sat down upon the bones. When at last the clanking subsided, I resumed the trowel, and finished without interruption the fifth, the sixth, and the seventh tier. The wall was now nearly upon a level with my breast. I again paused, and holding the flambeaux over the mason-work, threw a few feeble rays upon the figure within.

A succession of loud and shrill screams, bursting suddenly from the throat of the chained form, seemed to thrust me violently back. For a brief moment I hesitated—I trembled. Unsheathing my rapier, I began to grope with it about the recess; but the thought of an instant reassured me. I placed my hand upon the solid fabric of the catacombs, and felt satisfied. I re-approached the wall. I replied to the yells of him who clamoured. I re-echoed—I aided—I surpassed them in volume and in strength. I did this, and the clamourer grew still.

It was now midnight, and my task was drawing to a close. I had completed the eighth, the ninth, and the tenth tier. I had finished a portion of the last and the eleventh; there remained but a single stone to be fitted and plastered in. I struggled with its weight; I placed it partially in its destined position. But now there came from out the niche a low laugh that erected the hairs upon my head. It was succeeded by a sad voice, which I had difficulty in recognising as that of the noble Fortunato. The voice said—

"Ha! ha! ha!—he! he!—a very good joke indeed—an excellent jest. We will have many a rich laugh about it at the palazzo—he! he! he!—over our wine—he! he! he!"

"The Amontillado!" I said.

"He! he! he!—he! he! he!—yes, the Amontillado. But is it not getting late? Will not they be awaiting us at the palazzo, the Lady Fortunato and the rest? Let us be gone."

"Yes," I said, "let us be gone."

"For the love of God, Montresor!"

"Yes," I said, "for the love of God!"

But to these words I hearkened in vain for a reply. I grew impatient. I called aloud—

"Fortunato!"

No answer. I called again—

"Fortunato!"

No answer still. I thrust a torch through the remaining aperture and let it fall within. There came forth in return only a jingling of the bells. My heart grew sick—on account of the dampness of the catacombs. I hastened to make an end of my labour. I forced the last stone into its position; I plastered it up. Against the new masonry I re-erected the old rampart of bones. For the half of a century no mortal has disturbed them. *In pace requiescat!*

EARL BEARDIE'S
GAME AT CARDS

S CIENCE THAT HAS SWEPT AWAY, with its busy broom, so many picturesque cobwebs, has not interfered much with Glamis Castle. From that stronghold, legend and superstition grimly defy enlightenment, and fancy has only to play round the spot for some weird scene or other to flash forth. The mysterious room which everyone knows to exist, but of which only the Earl, the heir, and the factor of each generation know anything further, has, of course, been a treasure-trove of surmise, not only with the peasantry of the place, but with all who love the eerie.

Earl Beardie is the hero, and an ideal hero for the purpose. He was fierce and wild and wicked, and feared neither God nor man. As a consequence, everybody feared him, and opposition to his will was a thing he had seldom to brook. But one memorable Sunday it met him. His views on the Sabbath—since largely adopted!—were rather too liberal for his day. He lived before his time, and had to pay the price of advancement. As a Scot among Scots, he could not but "remember the Sabbath Day," but it was only to keep it unholy. Hunting was, perforce, suspended (for what Scotch hounds would run of a Sunday?), but the more private desecration of a game at cards it grieved his spirit to forego.

It was a stormy November night. The ladies were at prayers, an exercise at which not even the wicked Earl cared to disturb them. With the cards in his hand, his problem was to find a partner.

One after another the domestics were summoned, but not even their terrible master could bully them into the direct transaction with Satan which handling "Deevil's bricks" on the Sabbath meant. Whereupon the raging Earl mounted to his turret-room and slammed the door behind him, vowing he would play with the Prince of Darkness himself, rather than relinquish his game.

The evil Fates were kind. Even as he spoke a tap came to the door, and a tall, dark stranger, cloaked and bonneted, presented himself in silence. Little cared the Earl for name or address. He had got what he wanted, and asked no questions. The cards were shuffled and dealt, and the game began.

Soon the trembling menials heard oaths and altercation, from which their experience led them to conclude that their master was losing. And losing indeed he was, so heavily, that soon he had nothing left to stake. "Make out what bond you will," he cried recklessly, "and I will sign without regarding it!" The stranger did so, the Earl signed, and with oaths and curses the game proceeded. At last the din inside grew so terrible, that the old family butler felt impelled to peep through the keyhole. The action was courageous but unwise. He fell back howling, and next instant the door was flung open, and the Earl appeared with a drawn sword.

"Stop him! Slay him!" he gasped. But the mysterious stranger was gone, and gone was the bond likewise. All that the Earl could tell was that his partner had glanced up suddenly, and exclaiming, "Smite that eye!" had disappeared in a streak of lightning through the keyhole. The butler's eye, long bruised and yellow-rimmed, bore out the tale.

It was five years before the bond was paid; and then, in the storms and winds of another wild November night, the Devil came to claim his own.

But though the body of Earl Beardie ceased from troubling, his spirit was as busy as ever. Each Sunday, as it came round, was made hideous by ghostly carousals in the turret. When the noises could be endured no longer, the room was stoutly walled up, and inside sit Earl Beardie and his partner playing cards till the crack of doom.

FRANKENSTEIN

Frankenstein is a young Genevese of good parentage. He is warmly attached to his family, which consists of a father, two brothers, named William and Ernest, and an adopted sister, Elizabeth Lavenza, to whom he is betrothed. He early displays a bent for natural science, to which he devotes his student years. He tells his own story.

O NE OF THE PHENOMENA which had peculiarly attracted my attention was the structure of the human frame, and, indeed, any animal endued with life. Whence, I often asked myself, did the principle of life proceed? It was a bold question, and one which has ever been considered as a mystery; yet with how many things are we upon the brink of becoming acquainted, if cowardice or carelessness did not restrain our inquiries. I revolved these circumstances in my mind, and determined thenceforth to apply myself more particularly to those branches of natural philosophy which relate to physiology. Unless I had been animated by an almost supernatural enthusiasm, my application to this study would have been irksome, and almost intolerable. To examine the causes of life, we must first have recourse to death. I became acquainted with the science of anatomy: but this was not sufficient; I must also observe the natural decay and corruption of the human body. In my education my father had taken the greatest precautions that my mind should be impressed with no supernatural horrors. I do not ever remember to have trembled at a tale of superstition, or to have feared the apparition of a spirit. Darkness had no effect upon my fancy; and a churchyard was to me merely the receptacle of bodies deprived of life, which, from being the seat of beauty and strength, had become food for the worm. Now I was led to examine the cause and progress of this decay, and forced to spend days and nights in vaults and charnel-houses. My attention was fixed upon every object the most insupportable to the delicacy of the human feelings. I saw how the fine form of man was degraded and wasted; I beheld the corruption of death succeed to the blooming cheek of life; I saw how the worm inherited the wonders of the eye and brain. I paused, examining and analysing all the minutiæ of causation, as exemplified in the change from life to death, and death to life, until from the midst of this darkness a sudden light broke in upon me—a light so brilliant and wondrous, yet so simple, that while I became dizzy with the immensity of the prospect which it illustrated, I was surprised, that among so many men of genius who had directed their inquiries towards the same science, that I alone should be reserved to discover so astonishing a secret.

Remember, I am not recording the vision of a madman. The sun does not more certainly shine in the heavens, than that which I now affirm is true. Some miracle might have produced it, yet the stages of the discovery were distinct and probable. After days and nights of incredible labour and fatigue, I succeeded in discovering the cause of generation and life; nay, more, I became myself capable of bestowing animation upon lifeless matter.

The astonishment which I had at first experienced on this discovery soon gave place to delight and rapture. After so much time spent in painful labour, to arrive at once at the summit of my desires, was the most gratifying consummation of my toils. But this discovery was so great and overwhelming, that all the steps by which I had been progressively led to it were obliterated, and I beheld only the result. What had been the study and desire of the wisest men since the creation of the world was now within my grasp. Not that, like a magic scene, it all opened upon me at once: the information I had obtained was of a nature rather to direct my endeavours so soon as I should point them towards the object of my search, than to exhibit that object already accomplished. I was like the Arabian who had been buried with the dead, and found a passage to life, aided only by one glimmering, and seemingly ineffectual, light.

* * *

When I found so astonishing a power placed within my hands, I hesitated a long time concerning the manner in which I should employ it. Although I possessed the capacity of bestowing animation, yet to prepare a frame for the reception of it, with all its intricacies of fibres, muscles, and veins, still remained a work of inconceivable difficulty and labour. I doubted at first whether I should attempt the creation of a being like myself, or one of simpler organisation; but my imagination was too much exalted by my first success to permit me to doubt of my ability to give life to an animal as complex and wonderful as man. The materials at present within my command hardly appeared adequate to so arduous an undertaking; but I doubted not that I should ultimately succeed. I prepared myself for a multitude of reverses: my operations might be incessantly baffled, and at last my work be imperfect: yet, when I considered the improvement which every day takes place in science and mechanics, I was encouraged to hope my present attempts would at least lay the foundations of future success. Nor could I consider the magnitude and complexity of my plan as any argument of its impracticability. It was with these feelings that I began the creation of a human being. As the minuteness of the parts formed a great hindrance to my speed, I resolved, contrary to my first intention, to make the being of a gigantic stature—that is to say, about eight feet in height, and proportionably large. After having formed this determination, and having spent some months in successfully collecting and arranging my materials, I began.

No one can conceive the variety of feelings which bore me onwards, like a hurricane, in the first enthusiasm of success. Life and death appeared to me ideal bounds, which I should first break through, and pour a torrent of light into our dark world. A new species would bless me as its creator and source; many happy and excellent natures would owe their being to me. No father could claim the gratitude of his child so completely as I should deserve theirs. Pursuing these reflections, I thought, that if I could bestow animation upon lifeless matter, I might in process of time (although I now found it impossible) renew life where death had apparently devoted the body to corruption.

* * *

It was on a dreary night of November that I beheld the accomplishment of my toils. With an anxiety that almost amounted to agony, I collected the instruments of life around me, that I might infuse a spark of being into the lifeless thing that lay at my feet. It was already one in the morning; the rain pattered dismally against the panes, and my candle was nearly burnt out, when, by the glimmer of the half-extinguished light, I saw the dull yellow eye of the creature open; it breathed hard, and a convulsive motion agitated its limbs.

How can I describe my emotions at this catastrophe, or how delineate the wretch whom, with such infinite pains and care, I had endeavoured to form? His limbs were in proportion, and I had selected his features as beautiful. Beautiful!—Great God! His yellow skin scarcely covered the work of muscles and arteries beneath; his hair was of a lustrous black, and flowing; his teeth of a pearly whiteness; but these luxuriances only formed a more horrid contrast with his watery eyes, that seemed almost of the same colour as the dun white sockets in which they were set, his shrivelled complexion and straight black lips.

The different accidents of life are not so changeable as the feelings of human nature. I had worked hard for nearly two years, for the sole purpose of infusing life into an inanimate body. For this I had deprived myself of rest and health. I had desired it with an ardour that far exceeded moderation; but now that I had finished, the beauty of the dream vanished, and breathless horror and disgust filled my heart. Unable to endure the aspect of the being I had created, I rushed out of the room, and continued a long time traversing my bedchamber, unable to compose my mind to sleep. At length lassitude succeeded to the tumult I had before endured; and I threw myself on the bed in my clothes, endeavouring to seek a few moments of forgetfulness. But it was in vain: I slept, indeed, but I was disturbed by the wildest dreams. I thought I saw Elizabeth, in the bloom of health, walking in the streets of Ingolstadt. Delighted and surprised, I embraced her; but as I imprinted the first kiss on her lips, they became livid with the hue of death; her features appeared to change, and I thought that I held the corpse of my dead mother in my arms; a shroud enveloped her form, and I saw the grave-worms crawling in the folds of the flannel. I started from my sleep with horror; a cold dew covered my forehead, my teeth chattered, and every limb became convulsed: when, by the dim and yellow light of the moon, as it forced its way through the window shutters, I beheld the wretch—the miserable monster whom I had created. He held up the curtain of the bed; and his eyes, if eyes they may be called, were fixed on me. His jaws opened, and he muttered some inarticulate sounds, while a grin wrinkled his cheeks. He might have spoken, but I did not hear; one hand was stretched out, seemingly to detain me, but I escaped, and rushed downstairs. I took refuge in the courtyard belonging to the house which I inhabited, where I remained during the rest of the night, walking up and down in the greatest agitation, listening attentively, catching and fearing each sound as if it were to announce the approach of the demoniacal corpse to which I had so miserably given life.

Oh! no mortal could support the horror of that counte-nance. A mummy again endued with animation could not be so hideous as that wretch. I had gazed on him while unfinished; he was ugly then; but when those muscles and joints were rendered capable of motion, it became a thing such as even Dante could not have conceived.

I passed the night wretchedly. Sometimes my pulse beat so quickly and hardly, that I felt the palpitation of every artery; at others, I nearly sank to the ground through languor and extreme weakness. Mingled with this horror, I felt the bitter-ness of disappointment; dreams that had been my food and pleasant rest for so long a space were now become a hell to me; and the change was so rapid, the overthrow so complete!

Morning, dismal and wet, at length dawned, and dis-covered to my sleepless and aching eyes the church of Ingolstadt, its white steeple and clock, which indicated the sixth hour. The porter opened the gates of the court, which had that night been my asylum, and I issued into the streets, pacing them with quick steps, as if I sought to avoid the wretch whom I feared every turning of the street would present to my view. I did not dare return to the apartment which I inhabited, but felt impelled to hurry on, although drenched by the rain which poured from a black and comfortless sky.

I continued walking in this manner for some time, endeavouring, by bodily exercise, to ease the load that weighed upon my mind. I traversed the streets, without any clear conception of where I was, or what I was doing. My heart palpitated in the sickness of fear; and I hurried on with irregular steps, not daring to look about me.

He meets his friend, Henry Clerval, who returns with him and nurses him through an attack of brain-fever. Nothing is seen of the monster. Some months after his recovery he receives the following letter:—

"My dear Victor,—You have probably waited impatiently for a letter to fix the date of your return to us; and I was at first tempted to write only a few lines, merely mentioning the day on which I should expect you. But that would be a cruel kindness, and I dare not do it. What would be your surprise, my son, when you expected a happy and glad welcome, to behold, on the contrary, tears and wretchedness? And how, Victor, can I relate our misfortune? Absence cannot have rendered you callous to our joys and griefs; and how shall I inflict pain on my long absent son? I wish to prepare you for the woeful news, but I know it is impossible; even now your eye skims over the page, to seek the words which are to convey to you the horrible tidings.

"William is dead!—that sweet child, whose smiles delighted and warmed my heart, who was so gentle, yet so gay! Victor, he is murdered!

"I will not attempt to console you; but will simply relate the circumstances of the transaction.

"Last Thursday (May 7th), I, my niece, and your two brothers, went to walk in Plainpalais. The evening was warm and serene, and we prolonged our walk farther than usual. It was already dusk before we thought of returning; and then we discovered that William and Ernest, who had gone on before, were not to be found. We accordingly rested on a seat until they should return. Presently Ernest came, and inquired if we had seen his brother: he said, that he had been playing with him, that William had run away to hide himself, and that he vainly sought for him, and afterwards waited for him a long time, but that he did not return.

"This account rather alarmed us, and we continued to search for him until night fell, when Elizabeth conjectured that he might have returned to the house. He was not there. We returned again, with torches; for I could not rest, when I thought that my sweet boy had lost himself, and was exposed to all the damps and dews of night; Elizabeth also suffered extreme anguish. About five in the morning I discovered my lovely boy, whom the night before I had seen blooming and active in health, stretched on the grass livid and motionless: the print of the murderer's finger was on his neck.

"He was conveyed home, and the anguish that was visible in my countenance betrayed the secret to Elizabeth. She was very earnest to see the corpse. At first I attempted to prevent her; but she persisted, and entering the room where it lay, hastily examined the neck of the victim, and clasping her hands exclaimed, 'O God! I have murdered my darling child!'

"She fainted, and was restored with extreme difficulty. When she again lived, it was only to weep and sigh. She told me, that that same evening William had teased her to let him wear a very valuable miniature that she possessed of your mother. This picture is gone, and was doubtless the temptation which urged the murderer to the deed. We have no trace of him at present, although our exertions to discover him are unremitted; but they will not restore my beloved William!

"Come, dearest Victor; you alone can console Elizabeth. She weeps continually, and accuses herself unjustly as the cause of his death; her words pierce my heart. We are all unhappy; but will not that be an additional motive for you, my son, to return and be our comforter? Your dear mother! Alas, Victor! I now say, Thank God she did not live to witness the cruel, miserable death of her youngest darling!

"Come, Victor; not brooding thoughts of vengeance against the assassin, but with feelings of peace and gentleness, that will heal, instead of festering, the wounds of our minds. Enter the house of mourning, my friend, but with kindness and affection for those who love you, and not with hatred for your enemies.—Your affectionate and afflicted father,

"Alphonse Frankenstein.

"Geneva, May 12, 17—."

* * *

It was completely dark when I arrived in the environs of Geneva; the gates of the town were already shut; and I was obliged to pass the night at Secheron, a village at the distance of half a league from the city. The sky was serene; and, as I was unable to rest, I resolved to visit the spot where my poor William had been murdered. As I could not pass through the town, I was obliged to cross the lake in a boat to arrive at Plainpalais. During this short voyage I saw the lightnings played on the summit of Mont Blanc in the most beautiful figures. The storm appeared to approach rapidly; and, on landing, I ascended a low hill, that I might observe its progress. It advanced; the heavens were clouded, and I soon felt the rain coming slowly in large drops, but its violence quickly increased.

I quitted my seat, and walked on, although the darkness and storm increased every minute, and the thunder burst with a terrific crash over my head. It was echoed from Salève, the Juras, and the Alps of Savoy; vivid flashes of lightning dazzled my eyes, illuminating the lake, making it appear like a vast sheet of fire; then for an instant everything seemed of a pitchy darkness, until the eye recovered itself from the preceding flash. The storm, as is often the case in Switzerland, appeared at once in various parts of the heavens. The most violent storm hung exactly north of the town, over that part of the lake which lies between the promontory of Belrive and the village of Copêt. Another storm enlightened Jura with faint flashes; and another darkened and sometimes disclosed the Môle, a peaked mountain to the east of the lake.

While I watched the tempest, so beautiful yet terrific, I wandered on with a hasty step. This noble war in the sky elevated my spirits; I clasped my hands, and exclaimed aloud, "William, dear angel! this is thy funeral, this thy dirge!" As I said these words, I perceived in the gloom a figure which stole from behind a clump of trees near me; I stood fixed, gazing intently: I could not be mistaken. A flash of lightning illuminated the object, and discovered its shape plainly to me; its gigantic stature, and the deformity of its aspect, more hideous than belongs to humanity, instantly informed me that it was the wretch, the filthy dæmon, to whom I had given life. What did he there? Could he be (I shuddered at the conception) the murderer of my brother? No sooner did that idea cross my imagination, than I became convinced of its truth; my teeth chattered, and I was forced to lean against a tree for support. The figure passed me quickly, and I lost it in the gloom. Nothing in human shape could have destroyed that fair child. He was the murderer! I could not doubt it. The mere presence of the idea was an irresistible proof of the fact. I thought of pursuing the devil; but it would have been in vain, for another flash discovered him to me hanging among the rocks of the nearly perpendicular ascent of Mont Salêve, a hill that bounds Plainpalais on the south. He soon reached the summit, and disappeared.

I remained motionless. The thunder ceased; but the rain still continued, and the scene was enveloped in an impenetrable darkness. I revolved in my mind the events which I had until now sought to forget: the whole train of my progress towards the creation; the appearance of the work of my own hands alive at my bedside; its departure. Two years had now nearly elapsed since the night on which he first received life; and was this his first crime? Alas! I had turned loose into the world a depraved wretch, whose delight was in carnage and misery; had he not murdered my brother?

No one can conceive the anguish I suffered during the remainder of the night, which I spent, cold and wet, in the open air. But I did not feel the inconvenience of the weather; my imagination was busy in scenes of evil and despair. I considered the being whom I had cast among mankind, and endowed with the will and power to effect purposes of horror, such as the deed which he had now done, nearly in the light of my own vampire, my own spirit let loose from the grave, and forced to destroy all that was dear to me.

Justine, an innocent individual, is charged with the murder, and executed on circumstantial evidence. Frankenstein, wandering in agony of mind among the mountains, is again encountered by the monster, who tells his story.

"It is with considerable difficulty that I remember the original era of my being: all the events of that period appear confused and indistinct. A strange multiplicity of sensations seized me, and I saw, felt, heard, and smelt, at the same time; and it was, indeed, a long time before I learned to distinguish between the operations of my various senses. By degrees, I remember, a stronger light pressed upon my nerves, so that I was obliged to shut my eyes. Darkness then came over me, and troubled me; but hardly had I felt this, when, by opening my eyes, as I now suppose, the light poured in upon me again. I walked, and I believe, descended; but I presently found a great alteration in my sensations. Before, dark and opaque bodies had surrounded me, impervious to my touch or sight; but I now found that I could wander on at liberty, with no obstacles which I could not either surmount or avoid. The light became more and more oppressive to me; and, the heat wearying me as I walked, I sought a place where I could receive shade. This was a forest near Ingolstadt; and here I lay by the side of a brook resting from my fatigue, until I felt tormented by hunger and thirst. This roused me from my nearly dormant state, and I ate some berries which I found hanging on the trees, or lying on the ground. I slaked my thirst at the brook; and then lying down, was overcome by sleep.

"It was dark when I awoke; I felt cold also, and half-frightened, as it were instinctively, finding myself so desolate. Before I had quitted your apartment, on a sensation of cold, I had covered myself with some clothes; but these were insufficient to secure me from the dews of night. I was a poor, helpless, miserable wretch; I knew, and could distinguish, nothing; but feeling pain invade me on all sides, I sat down and wept.

"Soon a gentle light stole over the heavens, and gave me a sensation of pleasure. I started up, and beheld a radiant form rise from among the trees.[*] I gazed with a kind of wonder. It moved slowly, but it enlightened my path; and I again went out in search of berries. I was still cold, when under one of the trees I found a huge cloak, with which I covered myself, and sat down upon the ground. No distinct ideas occupied my mind; all was confused. I felt light, and hunger, and thirst, and darkness; innumerable sounds rung in my ears, and on all sides various scents saluted me; the only object that I could distinguish was the bright moon, and I fixed my eyes on that with pleasure.

---

[*] The Moon.

"Several changes of day and night passed, and the orb of night had greatly lessened, when I began to distinguish my sensations from each other. I gradually saw plainly the clear stream that supplied me with drink, and the trees that shaded me with their foliage. I was delighted when I first discovered that a pleasant sound, which often saluted my ears, proceeded from the throats of the little winged animals who had often intercepted the light from my eyes. I began also to observe, with greater accuracy, the forms that surrounded me, and to perceive the boundaries of the radiant roof of light which canopied me. Sometimes I tried to imitate the pleasant songs of the birds, but was unable. Sometimes I wished to express my sensations in my own mode, but the uncouth and inarticulate sounds which broke from me frightened me into silence again.

"The moon had disappeared from the night, and again, with a lessened form, showed itself, while I still remained in the forest. My sensations had, by this time, become distinct, and my mind received every day additional ideas. My eyes became accustomed to the light, and to perceive objects in their right forms; I distinguished the insect from the herb, and, by degrees, one herb from another. I found that the sparrow uttered none but harsh notes, whilst those of the blackbird and thrush were sweet and enticing.

"One day, when I was oppressed by cold, I found a fire which had been left by some wandering beggars, and was overcome with delight at the warmth I experienced from it. In my joy I thrust my hand into the live embers, but quickly drew it out again with a cry of pain. How strange, I thought, that the same cause should produce such opposite effects! I examined the materials of the fire, and to my joy found it to be composed of wood. I quickly collected some branches; but they were wet, and would not burn. I was pained at this, and sat still watching the operation of the fire. The wet wood which I had placed near the heat dried, and itself became inflamed. I reflected on this; and, by touching the various branches, I discovered the cause, and busied myself in collecting a great quantity of wood, that I might dry it, and have a plentiful supply of fire. When night came on, and brought sleep with it, I was in the greatest fear lest my fire should be extinguished. I covered it carefully with dry wood and leaves, and placed wet branches upon it; and then, spreading my cloak, I lay on the ground, and sunk into sleep.

"It was morning when I awoke, and my first care was to visit the fire. I uncovered it, and a gentle breeze quickly fanned it into a flame. I observed this also, and contrived a fan of branches, which roused the embers when they were nearly extinguished. When night came again, I found, with pleasure, that the fire gave light as well as heat; and that the discovery of this element was useful to me in my food; for I found some of the offals that the travellers had left had been roasted, and tasted much more savoury than the berries I gathered from the trees. I tried, therefore, to dress my food in the same manner, placing it on the live embers. I found that the berries were spoiled by this operation, and the nuts and roots much improved.

"Food, however, became scarce; and I often spent the whole day searching in vain for a few acorns to assuage the pangs of hunger. When I found this, I resolved to quit the place that I had hitherto inhabited, to seek for one where the few wants I experienced would be more easily satisfied. In this emigration, I exceedingly lamented the loss of the fire which I had obtained through accident, and knew not how to reproduce it. I gave several hours to the serious consideration of this difficulty; but I was obliged to relinquish all attempt to supply it; and, wrapping myself up in my cloak, I struck across the wood towards the setting sun. I passed three days in these rambles, and at length discovered the open country. A great fall of snow had taken place the night before, and the fields were of one uniform white; the appearance was disconsolate, and I found my feet chilled by the cold damp substance that covered the ground.

"It was about seven in the morning, and I longed to obtain food and shelter; at length I perceived a small hut, on a rising ground, which had doubtless been built for the convenience of some shepherd. This was a new sight to me; and I examined the structure with great curiosity.

Finding the door open, I entered. An old man sat in it, near a fire, over which he was preparing his breakfast. He turned on hearing a noise; and, perceiving me, shrieked loudly, and, quitting the hut, ran across the fields with a speed of which his debilitated form hardly appeared capable. His appearance, different from any I had ever before seen, and his flight, somewhat surprised me. But I was enchanted by the appearance of the hut: here the snow and rain could not penetrate: the ground was dry; and it presented to me then as exquisite and divine a retreat as Pandæmonium appeared to the dæmons of hell after their sufferings in the lake of fire. I greedily devoured the remnants of the shepherd's breakfast, which consisted of bread, cheese, milk, and wine; the latter, however, I did not like. Then, overcome by fatigue, I lay down among some straw, and fell asleep.

"It was noon when I awoke; and, allured by the warmth of the sun, which shone brightly on the white ground, I determined to recommence my travels; and, depositing the remains of the peasant's breakfast in a wallet I found, I proceeded across the fields for several hours, until at sunset I arrived at a village. How miraculous did this appear! the huts, the neater cottages, and stately houses, engaged my admiration by turns. The vegetables in the gardens, the milk and cheese that I saw placed at the windows of some of the cottages, allured my appetite.

"One of the best of these I entered; but I had hardly placed my foot within the door, before the children shrieked, and one of the women fainted. The whole village was roused; some fled, some attacked me, until, grievously bruised by stones and many other kinds of missile weapons, I escaped to the open country, and fearfully took refuge in a low hovel, quite bare, and making a wretched appearance after the palaces I had beheld in the village. This hovel, however, joined a cottage of a neat and pleasant appearance; but, after my late dearly bought experience, I dared not enter it. My place of refuge was constructed of wood, but so low, that I could with difficulty sit upright in it. No wood, however, was placed on the earth which formed the floor, but it was dry; and although the wind entered it by innumerable chinks, I found it an agreeable asylum from the snow and rain.

"Here then I retreated, and lay down happy to have found a shelter, however miserable, from the inclemency of the season, and still more from the barbarity of man.

"As soon as morning dawned, I crept from my kennel, that I might view the adjacent cottage, and discover if I could remain in the habitation I had found. It was situated against the back of the cottage, and surrounded on the sides which were exposed by a pig-sty and a clear pool of water. One part was open, and by that I had crept in; but now I covered every crevice by which I might be perceived with stones and wood, yet in such a manner that I might move them on occasion to pass out: all the light I enjoyed came through the sty, and that was sufficient for me.

"Having thus arranged my dwelling, and carpeted it with clean straw, I retired; for I saw the figure of a man at a distance, and I remembered too well my treatment the night before, to trust myself in his power. I had first, however, provided for my sustenance for that day, by a loaf of coarse bread, which I purloined, and a cup with which I could drink, more conveniently than from my hand, of the pure water which flowed by my retreat The floor was a little raised, so that it was kept perfectly dry, and by its vicinity to the chimney of the cottage it was tolerably warm.

"Being thus provided, I resolved to reside in this hovel, until something should occur which might alter my determination. It was indeed a paradise, compared to the bleak forest, my former residence, the rain-dropping branches, and dank earth. I ate my breakfast with pleasure, and was about to remove a plank to procure myself a little water, when I heard a step, and looking through a small chink, I beheld a young creature, with a pail on her head, passing before my hovel. The girl was young, and of gentle demeanour, unlike what I have since found cottagers and farm-house servants to be. Yet she was meanly dressed, a coarse blue petticoat and a linen jacket being her only garb; her fair hair was plaited, but not adorned: she looked patient, yet sad. I lost sight of her; and in about a quarter of an hour she returned, bearing the pail, which was now partly filled with milk. As she walked along, seemingly incommoded by the burden, a young man met her, whose countenance expressed a deeper despondence. Uttering a few sounds with an air of melancholy, he took the pail from her head, and bore it to the cottage himself. She followed, and they disappeared. Presently I saw the young man again, with some tools in his hand, cross the field behind the cottage; and the girl was also busied, sometimes in the house, and sometimes in the yard.

"On examining my dwelling, I found that one of the windows of the cottage had formerly occupied a part of it, but the panes had been filled up with wood. In one of these was a small and almost imperceptible chink, through which the eye could just penetrate. Through this crevice a small room was visible, whitewashed and clean, but very bare of furniture. In one corner, near a small fire, sat an old man, leaning his head on his hands in a disconsolate attitude. The young girl was occupied in arranging the cottage: but presently she took something out of a drawer, which employed her hands, and she sat down beside the old man, who, taking up an instrument, began to play, and to produce sounds sweeter than the voice of the thrush or the nightingale. It was a lovely sight, even to me, poor wretch! who had never beheld aught beautiful before.

The silver hair and benevolent countenance of the aged cottager won my reverence, while the gentle manners of the girl enticed my love. He played a sweet mournful air, which I perceived drew tears from the eyes of his amiable companion, of which the old man took no notice, until she sobbed audibly; he then pronounced a few sounds, and the fair creature, leaving her work, knelt at his feet. He raised her, and smiled with such kindness and affection, that I felt sensations of a peculiar and overpowering nature: they were a mixture of pain and pleasure, such as I had never before experienced, either from hunger or cold, warmth or food; and I withdrew from the window, unable to bear these emotions.

"Soon after this the young man returned, bearing on his shoulders a load of wood. The girl met him at the door, helped to relieve him of his burden, and, taking some of the fuel into the cottage, placed it on the fire: then she and the youth went apart into a nook of the cottage, and he showed her a large loaf and piece of cheese. She seemed pleased, and went into the garden for some roots and plants, which she placed in water, and then upon the fire. She afterwards continued her work, whilst the young man went into the garden, and appeared busily employed in digging and pulling up roots. After he had been employed thus about an hour, the young woman joined him, and they entered the cottage together.

"The old man had, in the meantime, been pensive; but, on the appearance of his companions, he assumed a more cheerful air, and they sat down to eat. The meal was quickly despatched. The young woman was again occupied in arranging the cottage; the old man walked before the cottage in the sun for a few minutes, leaning on the arm of the youth. Nothing could exceed in beauty the contrast between these two excellent creatures. One was old, with silver hairs and a countenance beaming with benevolence and love; the younger was slight and graceful in his figure, and his features were moulded with the finest symmetry; yet his eyes and attitude expressed the utmost sadness and despondency. The old man returned to the cottage; and the youth, with tools different from those he had used in the morning, directed his steps across the fields.

"Night quickly shut in; but, to my extreme wonder, I found that the cottagers had a means of prolonging light by the use of tapers, and was delighted to find that the setting of the sun did not put an end to the pleasure I experienced in watching my human neighbours. In the evening the young girl and her companion were employed in various occupations which I did not understand; and the old man again took up the instrument which produced the divine sounds that had enchanted me in the morning. So soon as he had finished, the youth began, not to play, but to utter sounds that were monotonous, and neither resembling the harmony of the old man's instrument nor the songs of the birds: I since found that he read aloud, but at that time I knew nothing of the science of words or letters.

"The family, after having been thus occupied for a short time, extinguished their lights, and retired, as I conjectured, to rest."

When, after long secret observation, he has learnt to understand and adore this family, he discovers himself to them and begs their sympathy and protection. On being spurned with loathing excited by his gruesome appearance, he conceives a wild hatred for the whole human race. His one idea is, henceforth, revenge. The horror-stricken family fly from the cottage, which he burns to the ground. He then resumes his travels.

"In two months from this time I reached the environs of Geneva.

"It was evening when I arrived, and I retired to a hiding-place among the fields that surround it, to meditate in what manner I should apply to you. I was oppressed by fatigue and hunger, and far too unhappy to enjoy the gentle breezes of evening, or the prospect of the sun setting behind the stupendous mountains of Jura.

"At this time a slight sleep relieved me from the pain of reflection, which was disturbed by the approach of a beautiful child, who came running into the recess I had chosen, with all the sportiveness of infancy. Suddenly, as I gazed on him, an idea seized me, that this little creature was unprejudiced, and had lived too short a time to have imbibed a horror of deformity. If, therefore, I could seize him, and educate him as my companion and friend, I should not be so desolate in this peopled earth.

"Urged by this impulse, I seized on the boy as he passed, and drew him towards me. As soon as he beheld my form, he placed his hands before his eyes, and uttered a shrill scream: I drew his hand forcibly from his face, and said, 'Child, what is the meaning of this? I do not intend to hurt you; listen to me.'

"He struggled violently. 'Let me go,' he cried; 'monster! ugly wretch! you wish to eat me, and tear me to pieces—you are an ogre—let me go, or I will tell my papa.'

"'Boy, you will never see your father again; you must come with me.'

"'Hideous monster! let me go. My papa is a Syndic—he is M. Frankenstein—he will punish you. You dare not keep me.'

"'Frankenstein! you belong, then, to my enemy—to him towards whom I have sworn eternal revenge; you shall be my first victim.'

"The child still struggled, and loaded me with epithets which carried despair to my heart; I grasped his throat to silence him, and in a moment he lay dead at my feet

"I gazed on my victim, and my heart swelled with exultation and hellish triumph: clapping my hands, I exclaimed, 'I, too, can create desolation; my enemy is not invulnerable;

this death will carry despair to him, and a thousand other miseries shall torment and destroy him.'

"As I fixed my eyes on the child, I saw something glittering on his breast. I took it; it was a portrait of a most lovely woman. In spite of my malignity, it softened and attracted me. For a few moments I gazed with delight on her dark eyes, fringed by deep lashes, and her lovely lips; but presently my rage returned: I remembered that I was for ever deprived of the delights that such beautiful creatures could bestow; and that she whose resemblance I contemplated would, in regarding me, have changed that air of divine benignity to one expressive of disgust and affright.

"Can you wonder that such thoughts transported me with rage? I only wonder that at that moment, instead of venting my sensations in exclamations and agony, I did not rush among mankind and perish in the attempt to destroy them.

"While I was overcome by these feelings, I left the spot where I had committed the murder, and seeking a more secluded hiding-place, I entered a barn which had appeared to me to be empty. A woman was sleeping on some straw; she was young: not indeed so beautiful as her whose portrait I held; but of an agreeable aspect, and blooming in the loveliness of youth and health. Here, I thought, is one of those whose joy-imparting smiles are bestowed on all but me. And then I bent over her, and whispered, 'Awake, fairest, thy lover is near—he who would give his life but to obtain one look of affection from thine eyes: my beloved, awake!'

"The sleeper stirred; a thrill of terror ran through me. Should she indeed awake, and see me, and curse me, and denounce the murderer? Thus would she assuredly act, if her darkened eyes opened, and she beheld me. The thought was madness; it stirred the fiend within me—not I, but she shall suffer; the murder I have committed because I am for ever robbed of all that she could give me, she shall atone. The crime had its source in her: be hers the punishment! Thanks to the lessons of Felix and the sanguinary laws of man, I had learned now to work mischief. I bent over her, and placed the portrait securely in one of the folds of her dress. She moved again, and I fled.

"For some days I haunted the spot where these scenes had taken place; sometimes wishing to see you, sometimes resolved to quit the world and its miseries for ever. At length I wandered towards these mountains, and have ranged through their immense recesses, consumed by a burning passion which you alone can gratify. We may not part until you have promised to comply with my requisition. I am alone, and miserable; man will not associate with me; but one as deformed and horrible as myself would not deny herself to me. My companion must be of the same species, and have the same defects. This being you must create."

This Frankenstein at length, much against his will, consents to do; postponing his marriage with Elizabeth until it is accomplished. He sets about his task in one of the remotest of the Orkneys.

I sat one evening in my laboratory; the sun had set, and the moon was just rising from the sea; I had not sufficient light for my employment, and I remained idle, in a pause of consideration of whether I should leave my labour for the night, or hasten its conclusion by an unremitting attention to it. As I sat, a train of reflection occurred to me, which led me to consider the effects of what I was now doing. Three years before I was engaged in the same manner, and had created a fiend whose unparalleled barbarity had desolated my heart, and filled it for ever with the bitterest remorse. I was now about to form another being, of whose dispositions I was alike ignorant; she might become ten thousand times more malignant than her mate, and delight, for its own sake, in murder and wretchedness. He had sworn to quit the neighbourhood of man, and hide himself in deserts; but she had not; and she, who in all probability was to become a thinking and reasoning animal, might refuse to comply with a compact made before her creation. They might even hate each other; the creature who already lived loathed his own deformity, and might he not conceive a greater abhorrence for it when it came before his eyes in the female form? She also might turn with disgust from him to the superior beauty of man; she might quit him, and he be again alone, exasperated by the fresh provocation of being deserted by one of his own species.

Even if they were to leave Europe, and inhabit the deserts of the New World, yet one of the first results of those sympathies for which the dæmon thirsted would be children, and a race of devils would be propagated upon the earth, who might make the very existence of the species of man a condition precarious and full of terror. Had I right, for my own benefit, to inflict this curse upon everlasting generations? I had before been moved by the sophisms of the being I had created; I had been struck senseless by his fiendish threats; but now, for the first time, the wickedness of my promise burst upon me; I shuddered to think that future ages might curse me as their pest, whose selfishness had not hesitated to buy its own peace at the price, perhaps, of the existence of the whole human race.

I trembled, and my heart failed within me; when, on looking up, I saw, by the light of the moon, the dæmon at the casement. A ghastly grin wrinkled his lips as he gazed on me, where I sat fulfilling the task which he had allotted to me. Yes, he had followed me in my travels; he had loitered in forests, hid himself in caves, or taken refuge in wide and desert heaths; and he now came to mark my progress, and claim the fulfilment of my promise.

As I looked on him, his countenance expressed the utmost extent of malice and treachery. I thought with a sensation of madness on my promise of creating another like to him, and trembling with passion, tore to pieces the thing on which I was engaged. The wretch saw me destroy the creature on whose future existence he depended for happiness, and, with a howl of devilish despair and revenge, withdrew.

I left the room, and, locking the door, made a solemn vow in my own heart never to resume my labours; and then, with trembling steps, I sought my own apartment. I was alone; none were near me to dissipate the gloom, and relieve me from the sickening oppression of the most terrible reveries.

Several hours passed, and I remained near my window gazing on the sea; it was almost motionless, for the winds were hushed, and all nature reposed under the eye of the quiet moon. A few fishing vessels alone specked the water, and now and then the gentle breeze wafted the sound of voices, as the fishermen called to one another. I felt the silence, although I was hardly conscious of its extreme profundity, until my ear was suddenly arrested by the paddling of oars near the shore, and a person landed close to my house.

In a few minutes after, I heard the creaking of my door, as if someone endeavoured to open it softly. I trembled from head to foot; I felt a presentiment of who it was, and wished to rouse one of the peasants who dwelt in a cottage not far from mine; but I was overcome by the sensation of helplessness, so often felt in frightful dreams, when you in vain endeavour to fly from an impending danger, and was rooted to the spot.

Presently I heard the sound of footsteps along the passage; the door opened, and the wretch whom I dreaded appeared. Shutting the door, he approached me, and said, in a smothered voice—"You have destroyed the work which you began; what is it that you intend? Do you dare to break your promise? I have endured toil and misery; I left Switzerland with you; I crept along the shores of the Rhine, among its willow islands, and over the summits of its hills. I have dwelt many months in the heaths of England, and among the deserts of Scotland. I have endured incalculable fatigue and cold and hunger; do you dare destroy my hopes?"

"Begone! I do break my promise; never will I create another like yourself, equal in deformity and wickedness."

"Slave, I before reasoned with you, but you have proved yourself unworthy of my condescension. Remember that I have power; you believe yourself miserable, but I can make you so wretched that the light of day will be hateful to you. You are my creator, but I am your master;—obey!"

"The hour of my irresolution is past, and the period of your power is arrived. Your threats cannot move me to do an act of wickedness; but they confirm me in a determination of not creating you a companion in vice. Shall I, in cool blood, set loose upon the earth a dæmon, whose delight is in death and wretchedness? Begone! I am firm, and your words will only exasperate my rage."

The monster saw my determination in my face, and gnashed his teeth in the impotence of anger. "Shall each man," cried he, "find a wife for his bosom, and each beast have his mate, and I be alone? I had feelings of affection, and they were requited by detestation and scorn. Man! you may hate; but beware! your hours will pass in dread and misery, and soon the bolt will fall which must ravish from you your happiness for ever. Are you to be happy, while I grovel in the intensity of my wretchedness? You can blast my other passions; but revenge remains—revenge, henceforth dearer than light or food! I may die; but first you, my tyrant and tormentor, shall curse the sun that gazes on your misery. Beware; for I am fearless, and therefore powerful. I will watch with the wiliness of a snake, that I may sting with its venom. Man, you shall repent of the injuries you inflict."

"Devil, cease; and do not poison the air with these sounds of malice. I have declared my resolution to you, and I am no coward to bend beneath words. Leave me; I am inexorable."

"It is well. I go; but remember, I shall be with you on your wedding-night."

I started forward and exclaimed, "Villain! before you sign my death-warrant, be sure that you are yourself safe."

I would have seized him; but he eluded me, and quitted the house with precipitation. In a few moments I saw him in his boat, which shot across the waters with an arrowy swiftness, and was soon lost amidst the waves.

All was again silent; but his words rung in my ears. I burned with rage to pursue the murderer of my peace, and precipitate him into the ocean. I walked up and down my room hastily and perturbed, while my imagination conjured up a thousand images to torment and sting me. Why had I not followed him, and closed with him in mortal strife? But I had suffered him to depart, and he had directed his course towards the mainland. I shuddered to think who might be the next victim sacrificed to his insatiate revenge. And then I thought again of his words—"I will be with you on your wedding-night."

That then was the period fixed for the fulfilment of my destiny. In that hour I should die, and at once satisfy and extinguish his malice. The prospect did not move me to fear; yet when I thought of my beloved Elizabeth,—of her tears and endless sorrow, when she should find her lover so barbarously snatched from her,—tears, the first I had shed for many months, streamed from my eyes, and I resolved not to fall before my enemy without a bitter struggle.

He goes out alone in a skiff to rid himself of the unfinished body, and is driven by a storm to the Irish coast. There he is roughly received and taken before a magistrate.

I was soon introduced into the presence of the magistrate, an old benevolent man, with calm and mild manners. He looked upon me, however, with some degree of severity; and then, turning towards my conductors, he asked who appeared as witnesses on this occasion.

About half-a-dozen men came forward; and, one being selected by the magistrate, he deposed, that he had been out fishing the night before with his son and brother-in-law, Daniel Nugent, when, about ten o'clock, they observed a strong northerly blast rising, and they accordingly put in for port. It was a very dark night, as the moon had not yet risen; they did not land at the harbour, but, as they had been accustomed, at a creek about two miles below. He walked on first, carrying a part of the fishing tackle, and his companions followed him at some distance. As he was proceeding along the sands, he struck his foot against something, and fell at his length on the ground. His companions came up to assist him; and, by the light of their lantern, they found that he had fallen on the body of a man, who was to all appearance dead. Their first supposition was, that it was the corpse of some person who had been drowned, and was thrown on shore by the waves; but, on examination, they found that the clothes were not wet, and even that the body was not then cold. They instantly carried it to the cottage of an old woman near the spot, and endeavoured, but in vain, to restore it to life. It appeared to be a handsome young man, about five-and-twenty years of age. He had apparently been strangled; for there was no sign of any violence, except the black mark of fingers on his neck.

The first part of this deposition did not in the least interest me; but when the mark of the fingers was mentioned, I remembered the murder of my brother, and felt myself extremely agitated; my limbs trembled, and a mist came over my eyes, which obliged me to lean on a chair for support. The magistrate observed me with a keen eye, and of course drew an unfavourable augury from my manner.

The son confirmed his father's account; but when Daniel Nugent was called, he swore positively that, just before the fall of his companion, he saw a boat, with a single man in it, at a short distance from the shore; and, as far as he could judge by the light of a few stars, it was the same boat in which I had just landed.

A woman deposed that she lived near the beach, and was standing at the door of her cottage, waiting for the return of the fishermen, about an hour before she heard of the discovery of the body, when she saw a boat, with only one man in it, push off from that part of the shore where the corpse was afterwards found.

Another woman confirmed the account of the fishermen having brought the body into her house; it was not cold. They put it into a bed and rubbed it; and Daniel went to the town for an apothecary, but life was quite gone.

Several other men were examined concerning my landing; and they agreed that, with the strong north wind that had arisen during the night, it was very probable that I had beaten about for many hours, and had been obliged to return nearly to the same spot from which I had departed. Besides, they observed that it appeared that I had brought the body from another place, and it was likely, that as I did not appear to know the shore, I might have put into the harbour ignorant of the distance of the town of —— from the place where I had deposited the corpse.

Mr Kirwin, on hearing this evidence, desired that I should be taken into the room where the body lay for interment, that it might be observed what effect the sight of it would produce upon me. This idea was probably suggested by the extreme agitation I had exhibited when the mode of the murder had been described. I was accordingly conducted, by the magistrate and several other persons, to the inn. I could not help being struck by the strange coincidences that had taken place during this eventful night; but, knowing that I had been conversing with several persons in the island I had inhabited about the time that the body had been found, I was perfectly tranquil as to the consequences of the affair.

I entered the room where the corpse lay, and was led up to the coffin. How can I describe my sensations on beholding it? I feel yet parched with horror, nor can I reflect on that terrible moment without shuddering and agony. The examination, the presence of the magistrate and witnesses, passed like a dream from my memory, when I saw the lifeless form of Henry Clerval stretched before me. I gasped for breath; and, throwing myself on the body, I exclaimed, "Have my murderous machinations deprived you also, my dearest Henry, of life? Two I have already destroyed; other victims await their destiny: but you, Clerval, my friend, my benefactor—"

The human frame could no longer support the agonies that I endured, and I was carried out of the room in strong convulsions.

A fever succeeded to this. I lay for two months on the point of death; my ravings, as I afterwards heard, were frightful; I called myself the murderer of William, of Justine, and of Clerval. Sometimes I entreated my attendants to assist me in the destruction of the fiend by whom I was tormented; and at others, I felt the fingers of the monster already grasping my neck, and screamed aloud with agony and terror. Fortunately, as I spoke my native language, Mr Kirwin alone understood me; but my gestures and bitter cries were sufficient to affright the other witnesses.

Why did I not die? More miserable than man ever was before, why did I not sink into forgetfulness and rest? Death snatches away many blooming children, the only hopes of their doating parents: how many brides and youthful lovers have been one day in the bloom of health and hope, and the next a prey for worms and the decay of the tomb! Of what materials was I made, that I could thus resist so many shocks, which, like the turning of the wheel, continually renewed the torture?

He is acquitted on proving an alibi, and returns home.

In about a week after the arrival of Elizabeth's letter, we returned to Geneva. The sweet girl welcomed me with warm affection; yet tears were in her eyes, as she beheld my emaciated frame and feverish cheeks. I saw a change in her also. She was thinner, and had lost much of that heavenly vivacity that had before charmed me; but her gentleness, and soft looks of compassion, made her a more fit companion for one blasted and miserable as I was.

The tranquillity which I now enjoyed did not endure. Memory brought madness with it; and when I thought of what had passed, a real insanity possessed me; sometimes I was furious, and burnt with rage; sometimes low and despondent. I neither spoke, nor looked at any one, but sat motionless, bewildered by the multitude of miseries that overcame me.

Elizabeth alone had the power to draw me from these fits; her gentle voice would soothe me when transported by passion, and inspire me with human feelings when sunk in torpor. She wept with me, and for me. When reason returned, she would remonstrate, and endeavour to inspire me with resignation. Ah! it is well for the unfortunate to be resigned, but for the guilty there is no peace. The agonies of remorse poison the luxury there is otherwise sometimes found in indulging the excess of grief.

Soon after my arrival, my father spoke of my immediate marriage with Elizabeth. I remained silent.

"Have you then some other attachment?"

"None on earth. I love Elizabeth, and look forward to our union with delight. Let the day therefore be fixed; and on it I will consecrate myself, in life or death, to the happiness of my cousin."

"My dear Victor, do not speak thus. Heavy misfortunes have befallen us; but let us only cling closer to what remains, and transfer our love for those whom we have lost to those who yet live. Our circle will be small, but bound close by the ties of affection and mutual misfortune. And when time shall have softened your despair, new and dear objects of care will be born to replace those of whom we have been so cruelly deprived."

Such were the lessons of my father. But to me the remembrance of the threat returned: nor can you wonder, that, omnipotent as the fiend had yet been in his deeds of blood, I should almost regard him as invincible; and that when he had pronounced the words, "I shall be with you on your wedding-night," I should regard the threatened fate as unavoidable. But death was no evil to me, if the loss of Elizabeth were balanced with it; and I therefore, with a contented and even cheerful countenance, agreed with my father, that if my cousin would consent, the ceremony should take place in ten days, and thus put, as I imagined, the seal to my fate.

Great God! if for one instant I had thought what might be the hellish intention of my fiendish adversary, I would rather have banished myself for ever from my native country, and wandered a friendless outcast over the earth, than have consented to this miserable marriage. But, as if possessed of magic powers, the monster had blinded me to his real intentions; and when I thought that I had prepared only my own death, I hastened that of a far dearer victim.

As the period fixed for our marriage drew nearer, whether from cowardice or a prophetic feeling, I felt my heart sink within me. But I concealed my feelings by an appearance of hilarity, that brought smiles and joy to the countenance of my father, but hardly deceived the ever-watchful and nicer eye of Elizabeth. She looked forward to our union with placid contentment, not unmingled with a little fear, which past misfortunes had impressed, that what now appeared certain and tangible happiness, might soon dissipate into an airy dream, and leave no trace but deep and everlasting regret.

Preparations were made for the event; congratulatory visits were received; and all wore a smiling appearance. I shut up, as well as I could, in my own heart the anxiety that preyed there, and entered with seeming earnestness into the plans of my father, although they might only serve as the decorations of my tragedy. Through my father's exertions, a part of the inheritance of Elizabeth had been restored to her by the Austrian Government. A small possession on the shores of Como belonged to her. It was agreed that, immediately after our union, we should proceed to Villa Lavenza, and spend our first days of happiness beside the beautiful lake near which it stood.

In the meantime I took every precaution to defend my person, in case the fiend should openly attack me. I carried pistols and a dagger constantly about me, and was ever on the watch to prevent artifice; and by these means gained a greater degree of tranquillity. Indeed, as the period approached, the threat appeared more as a delusion, not to be regarded as worthy to disturb my peace, while the happiness I hoped for in my marriage wore a greater appearance of certainty, as the day fixed for its solemnisation drew nearer, and I heard it continually spoken of as an occurrence which no accident could possibly prevent.

Elizabeth seemed happy; my tranquil demeanour contributed greatly to calm her mind. But on the day that was to fulfil my wishes and my destiny, she was melancholy, and a presentiment of evil pervaded her; and perhaps also she thought of the dreadful secret which I had promised to reveal to her on the following day. My father was in the meantime overjoyed, and, in the bustle of preparation, only recognised in the melancholy of his niece the diffidence of a bride.

After the ceremony was performed, a large party assembled at my father's; but it was agreed that Elizabeth and I should commence our journey by water, sleeping that night at Evian, and continuing our voyage on the following day. The day was fair, the wind favourable, all smiled on our nuptial embarkation.

Those were the last moments of my life during which I enjoyed the feeling of happiness. We passed rapidly along: the sun was hot, but we were sheltered from its rays by a kind of canopy, while we enjoyed the beauty of the scene, sometimes on one side of the lake, where we saw Mont Salêve, the pleasant banks of Montalègre, and at a distance, surmounting all, the beautiful Mont Blanc, and the assemblage of snowy mountains that in vain endeavour to emulate her; sometimes coasting the opposite banks, we saw the mighty Jura opposing its dark side to the ambition that would quit its native country, and an almost insurmountable barrier to the invader who should wish to enslave it.

I took the hand of Elizabeth: "You are sorrowful, my love. Ah! if you knew what I have suffered, and what I may yet endure, you would endeavour to let me taste the quiet and freedom from despair, that this one day at least permits me to enjoy."

"Be happy, my dear Victor," replied Elizabeth; "there is, I hope, nothing to distress you; and be assumed that if a lively joy is not painted in my face, my heart is contented. Something whispers to me not to depend too much on the prospect that is opened before us; but I will not listen to such a sinister voice. Observe how fast we move along, and how the clouds, which sometimes obscure and sometimes rise above the dome of Mont Blanc, render this scene of beauty still more interesting. Look also at the innumerable fish that are swimming in the clear waters, where we can distinguish every pebble that lies at the bottom. What a divine day! how happy and serene all Nature appears!"

Thus Elizabeth endeavoured to divert her thoughts and mine from all reflection upon melancholy subjects. But her temper was fluctuating; joy for a few instants shone in her eyes, but it continually gave place to distraction and reverie.

The sun sunk lower in the heavens; we passed the river Drance, and observed its path through the chasms of the higher, and the glens of the lower, hills. The Alps here come closer to the lake, and we approached the amphi-theatre of mountains which forms its eastern boundary. The spire of Evian shone under the woods that surrounded it, and the range of mountain above mountain by which it was overhung.

The wind, which had hitherto carried us along with amazing rapidity, sunk at sunset to a light breeze; the soft air just ruffled the water, and caused a pleasant motion among the trees as we approached the shore, from which it wafted the most delightful scent of flowers and hay. The sun sunk beneath the horizon as we landed; and as I touched the shore, I felt those cares and fears revive, which soon were to clasp me, and cling to me for ever.

It was eight o'clock when we landed; we walked for a short time on the shore, enjoying the transitory light, and then retired to the inn, and contemplated the lovely scene of waters, woods, and mountains, obscured in darkness, yet still displaying their black outlines.

The wind, which had fallen in the south, now rose with great violence in the west. The moon had reached her summit in the heavens, and was beginning to descend; the clouds swept across it swifter than the flight of the vulture, and dimmed her rays, while the lake reflected the scene of the busy heavens, rendered still busier by the restless waves that were beginning to rise. Suddenly a heavy storm of rain descended.

I had been calm during the day; but so soon as night obscured the shapes of objects, a thousand fears arose in my mind. I was anxious and watchful, while my right hand grasped a pistol which was hidden in my bosom; every sound terrified me; but I resolved that I would sell my life dearly, and not shrink from the conflict until my own life, or that of my adversary, was extinguished.

Elizabeth observed my agitation for some time in timid and fearful silence; but there was something in my glance which communicated terror to her, and trembling she asked, "What is it that agitates you, my dear Victor? What is it you fear?"

"Oh! peace, peace, my love," replied I, "this night, and all will be safe: but this night is dreadful, very dreadful."

I passed an hour in this state of mind, when suddenly I reflected how fearful the combat which I momentarily expected would be to my wife, and I earnestly entreated her to retire, resolving not to join her until I had obtained some knowledge as to the situation of my enemy.

She left me, and I continued some time walking up and down the passages of the house, and inspecting every corner that might afford a retreat to my adversary. But I discovered no trace of him, and was beginning to conjecture that some fortunate chance had intervened to prevent the execution of his menaces; when suddenly I heard a shrill and dreadful scream. It came from the room into which Elizabeth had retired. As I heard it, the whole truth rushed into my mind, my arms dropped, the motion of every muscle and fibre was suspended; I could feel the blood trickling in my veins, and tingling in the extremities of my limbs. This state lasted but for an instant; the scream was repeated, and I rushed into the room.

Great God! why did I not then expire? Why am I here to relate the destruction of the best hope, and the purest creature of earth? She was there, lifeless and inanimate, thrown across the bed, her head hanging down, and her pale and distorted features half covered by her hair. Everywhere I turn I see the same figure—her bloodless arms and relaxed form flung by the murderer on its bridal bier. Could I behold this, and live? Alas! life is obstinate, and clings closest where it is most hated. For a moment only did I lose recollection; I fell senseless on the ground.

When I recovered, I found myself surrounded by the people of the inn; their countenances expressed a breathless terror; but the horror of others appeared only as a mockery, a shadow of the feelings that oppressed me. I escaped from them to the room where lay the body of Elizabeth, my love, my wife, so lately living, so dear, so worthy. She had been moved from the posture in which I had first beheld her; and now, as she lay, her head upon her arm, and a handkerchief thrown across her face and neck, I might have supposed her asleep. I rushed towards her, and embraced her with ardour; but the deadly languor and coldness of the limbs told me that what I now held in my arms had ceased to be the Elizabeth whom I had loved and cherished. The murderous mark of the fiend's grasp was on her neck, and the breath had ceased to issue from her lips.

While I still hung over her in the agony of despair, I happened to look up. The windows of the room had before been darkened, and I felt a kind of panic seeing the pale yellow light of the moon illuminate the chamber. The shutters had been thrown back; and with a sensation of horror not to be described, I saw at the open window a figure the most hideous and abhorred. A grin was on the face of the monster; he seemed to jeer, as with his fiendish finger he pointed towards the corpse of my wife. I rushed towards the window, and drawing a pistol from my bosom, fired; but he eluded me, leaped from his station, and, running with the swiftness of lightning, plunged into the lake.

The report of the pistol brought a crowd into the room. I pointed to the spot where he had disappeared, and we followed the track with boats; nets were cast, but in vain. After passing several hours, we returned hopeless, most of my companions believing it to have been a form conjured up by my fancy. After having landed, they proceeded to search the country, parties going in different directions among the woods and vines.

I attempted to accompany them, and proceeded a short distance from the house; but my head whirled round, my steps were like those of a drunken man, I fell at last in a state of utter exhaustion; a film covered my eyes, and my skin was parched with the heat of fever. In this state I was carried back, and placed on a bed, hardly conscious of what had happened; my eyes wandered round the room, as if to seek something that I had lost.

After an interval, I arose, as if by instinct, and crawled into the room where the corpse of my beloved lay. There were women weeping around—I hung over it, and joined my sad tears to theirs. All this time no distinct idea presented itself to my mind; but my thoughts rambled to various subjects, reflecting confusedly on my misfortunes, and their cause. I was bewildered in a cloud of wonder and horror. The death of William, the execution of Justine, the murder of Clerval, and lastly of my wife; even at that moment I knew not that my only remaining friends were safe from the malignity of the fiend; my father even now might be writhing under his grasp, and Ernest might be dead at his feet. This idea made me shudder, and recalled me to action. I started up, and resolved to return to Geneva with all possible speed.

There were no horses to be procured, and I must return by the lake; but the wind was unfavourable, and the rain fell in torrents. However, it was hardly morning, and I might reasonably hope to arrive by night. I hired men to row, and took an oar myself; for I had always experienced relief from mental torment in bodily exercise. But the overflowing misery I now felt, and the excess of agitation that I endured, rendered me incapable of any exertion. I threw down the oar; and leaning my head upon my hands, gave way to every gloomy idea that arose. If I looked up, I saw the scenes which were familiar to me in my happier time, and which I had contemplated but the day before in the company of her who was now but a shadow and a recollection. Tears streamed from my eyes. The rain had ceased for a moment, and I saw the fish play in the waters as they had done a few hours before; they had then been observed by Elizabeth. Nothing is so painful to the human mind as a great and sudden change. The sun might shine, or the clouds might lower; but nothing could appear to me as it had done the day before. A fiend had snatched from me every hope of future happiness: no creature had ever been so miserable as I was; so frightful an event is single in the history of man.

But why should I dwell upon the incidents that followed this last overwhelming event? Mine has been a tale of horrors; I have reached their acme, and what I must now relate can but be tedious to you. Know that, one by one, my friends were snatched away; I was left desolate. My own strength is exhausted; and I must tell, in a few words, what remains of my hideous narration.

I arrived at Geneva. My father and Ernest yet lived; but the former sunk under the tidings that I bore. I see him now, excellent and venerable old man! his eyes wandered in vacancy, for they had lost their charm and their delight—his Elizabeth, his more than daughter, whom he doated on with all that affection which a man feels, who in the decline of life, having few affections, clings more earnestly to those that remain. Cursed, cursed be the fiend that brought misery on his grey hairs, and doomed him to waste in wretchedness! He could not live under the horrors that were accumulated around him; the springs of existence suddenly gave way: he was unable to rise from his bed, and in a few days he died in my arms.

Frankenstein now devotes his life to the discovery and destruction of the monster. After a long pursuit, he almost tracks him down in the Arctic Ocean, but succumbs to the cold. He is rescued by a vessel en route for the North Pole, but which, finding it impossible to proceed, puts back to England, there extinguishing his last hope. He dies, and the man who is with him at the end, and to whom he has confided his history, relates the final episode.

I entered the cabin, where lay the remains of my ill-fated and admirable friend. Over him hung a form which I cannot find words to describe; gigantic in stature, yet uncouth and distorted in its proportions. As he hung over the coffin, his face was concealed by long locks of ragged hair; but one vast hand was extended, in colour and apparent texture like that of a mummy. When he heard the sound of my approach, he ceased to utter exclamations of grief and horror, and sprung towards the window. Never did I behold a vision so horrible as his face, of such loathsome, yet appalling hideousness. I shut my eyes involuntarily, and endeavoured to recollect what were my duties with regard to this destroyer. I called on him to stay.

He paused, looking on me with wonder; and, again turning towards the lifeless form of his creator, he seemed to forget my presence, and every feature and gesture seemed instigated by the wildest rage of some uncontrollable passion.

"That is also my victim!" he exclaimed: "in his murder my crimes are consummated; the miserable series of my being is wound to its close! Frankenstein! generous and self-devoted being! what does it avail that I now ask thee to pardon me? I, who irretrievably destroyed thee by destroying all thou lovedst. Alas! he is cold, he cannot answer me."

His voice seemed suffocated; and my first impulses, which had suggested to me the duty of obeying the dying request of my friend, in destroying his enemy, were now suspended by a mixture of curiosity and compassion. I approached this tremendous being; I dared not again raise my eyes to his face, there was something so scaring and unearthly in his ugliness. I attempted to speak, but the words died away on my lips. The monster continued to utter wild and incoherent self-reproaches. At length I gathered resolution to address him in a pause of the tempest of his passion: "Your repentance," I said, "is now superfluous. If you had listened to the voice of conscience, and heeded the stings of remorse, before you had urged your diabolical vengence to this extremity, Frankenstein would yet have lived."

"And do you dream," said the dæmon, "do you think that I was then dead to agony and remorse?—He," he continued, pointing to the corpse, "he suffered not in the consummation of the deed—oh! not the ten-thousandth portion of the anguish that was mine during the lingering detail of its execution. A frightful selfishness hurried me on, while my heart was poisoned with remorse. Think you that the groans of Clerval were music to my ears? My heart was fashioned to be susceptible of love and sympathy; and, when wrenched by misery to vice and hatred, it did not endure the violence of the change, without torture such as you cannot even imagine.

"After the murder of Clerval, I returned to Switzerland, heartbroken and overcome. I pitied Frankenstein; my pity amounted to horror: I abhorred myself. But when I discovered that he, the author at once of my existence and of its unspeakable torments, dared to hope for happiness; that while he accumulated wretchedness and despair upon me, he sought his own enjoyment in feelings and passions from the indulgence of which I was for ever barred, then impotent envy and bitter indignation filled me with an insatiable thirst for vengeance. I recollected my threat, and resolved that it should be accomplished. I knew that I was preparing for myself a deadly torture; but I was the slave, not the master, of an impulse which I detested, yet could not disobey. Yet when she died!—nay, then I was not miserable. I had cast off all feeling, subdued all anguish, to riot in the excess of my despair. Evil thenceforth became my good. Urged thus far, I had no choice but to adapt my nature to an element which I had willingly chosen. The completion of my demoniacal design became an insatiable passion. And now it is ended; there is my last victim."

I was at first touched by the expressions of his misery; yet, when I called to mind what Frankenstein had said of his powers of eloquence and persuasion, and when I again cast my eyes on the lifeless form of my friend, indignation was re-kindled within me.

"Wretch!" I said; "it is well that you come here to whine over the desolation that you have made. You throw a torch into a pile of buildings, and, when they are consumed, you sit among the ruins and lament the fall. Hypocritical fiend! if he whom you mourn still lived, still would he be the object, again would he become the prey, of your accursed vengeance. It is not pity that you feel; you lament only because the victim of your malignity is withdrawn from your power."

"Oh, it is not thus—not thus," interrupted the being; "yet such must be the impression conveyed to you by what appears to be the purport of my actions. Yet I seek not a fellow-feeling in my misery. No sympathy may I ever find. When I first sought it, it was the love of virtue, the feelings of happiness and affection with which my whole being overflowed, that I wished to be participated. But now that virtue has become to me a shadow, and that happiness and affection are turned into bitter and loathing despair, in what should I seek for sympathy? I am content to suffer alone, while my sufferings shall endure: when I die, I am well satisfied that abhorrence and opprobrium should load my memory. Once my fancy was soothed with dreams of virtue, of fame, and of enjoyment. Once I falsely hoped to meet with beings, who, pardoning my outward form, would love me for the excellent qualities which I was capable of unfolding. I was nourished with high thoughts of honour and devotion. But now crime has degraded me beneath the meanest animal. No guilt, no mischief, no malignity, no misery, can be found comparable to mine. When I run over the frightful catalogue of my sins, I cannot believe that I am the same creature whose thoughts were once filled with sublime and transcendent visions of the beauty and the majesty of goodness. But it is even so; the fallen angel becomes a malignant devil. Yet even that enemy of God and man had friends and associates in his desolation; I am alone.

"You, who call Frankenstein your friend, seem to have a knowledge of my crimes and his misfortunes. But in the detail which he gave you of them, he could not sum up the hours and months of misery which I endured, wasting in impotent passions. For while I destroyed his hopes, I did not satisfy my own desires. They were for ever ardent and craving; still I desired love and fellowship, and I was still spurned. Was there no injustice in this? Am I to be thought the only criminal, when all human kind sinned against me? Why do you not hate Felix, who drove his friend from his door with contumely? Why do you not execrate the rustic who sought to destroy the saviour of his child? Nay, these are virtuous and immaculate beings! I, the miserable and the abandoned, am an abortion, to be spurned at, and kicked, and trampled on. Even now my blood boils at the recollection of this injustice.

"But it is true that I am a wretch. I have murdered the lovely and the helpless; I have strangled the innocent as they slept, and grasped to death his throat who never injured me or any other living thing. I have devoted my creator, the select specimen of all that is worthy of love and admiration among men, to misery; I have pursued him even to that irremediable ruin. There he lies, white and cold in death. You hate me; but your abhorrence cannot equal that with which I regard myself. I look on the hands which executed the deed; I think on the heart in which the imagination of it was conceived, and long for the moment when these hands will meet my eyes, when that imagination will haunt my thoughts no more.

"Fear not that I shall be the instrument of future mischief. My work is nearly complete. Neither yours nor any man's death is needed to consummate the series of my being, and accomplish that which must be done; but it requires my own. Do not think I shall be slow to perform this sacrifice. I shall quit your vessel on the ice-raft which brought me thither, and shall seek the most northern extremity of the globe; I shall collect my funeral pile, and consume to ashes this miserable frame, that its remains may afford no light to any curious and unhallowed wretch, who would create such another as I have been. I shall die. I shall no longer feel the agonies which now consume me, or be the prey of feelings unsatisfied, yet unquenched. He is dead who called me into being; and when I shall be no more, the very remembrance of us will speedily vanish. I shall no longer see the sun or stars, or feel the winds play on my cheeks. Light, feeling, and sense will pass away; and in this condition must I find my happiness. Some years ago, when the images which this world affords first opened upon me, when I felt the cheering warmth of summer, and heard the rustling of the leaves and the warbling of the birds, and these were all to me, I should have wept to die; now it is my only consolation. Polluted by crimes, and torn by the bitterest remorse, where can I find rest but in death?

"Farewell! I leave you, and in you the last of human kind whom these eyes will ever behold. Farewell, Frankenstein! If thou wert yet alive, and yet cherished a desire of revenge against me, it would be better satiated in my life than in my destruction. But it was not so; thou didst seek my extinction, that I might not cause greater wretchedness; and if yet, in some mode unknown to me, thou hadst not ceased to think and feel, thou wouldst not desire against me a vengeance greater than that which I feel. Blasted as thou wert, my agony was still superior to thine; for the bitter sting of remorse will not cease to rankle in my wounds until death shall close them for ever.

"But soon," he cried, with sad and solemn enthusiasm, "I shall die, and what I now feel be no longer felt. Soon these burning miseries will be extinct. I shall ascend my funeral pile triumphantly, and exult in the agony of the torturing flames. The light of the conflagration will fade away: my ashes will be swept into the sea by the winds. My spirit will sleep in peace; or if it thinks, it will not surely think thus. Farewell."

He sprung from the cabin window, as he said this, upon the ice-raft which lay close to the vessel. He was soon borne away by the waves, and lost in darkness and distance.

THE GARDE CHASSE

WE RESIDED A GREAT DEAL on the Continent before I was married, and my mother had a favourite maid, named Françoise, who lived with her many years—a most trustworthy, excellent creature, in whom she had the greatest confidence; insomuch, that when I married, being very young and inexperienced, as she was obliged to separate from me herself, she transferred Françoise to my service, considering her better able to take care of me than anybody else.

I was living in Paris then, where Françoise, who was a native of Metz, had some relations settled in business, whom she often used to visit. She was generally very chatty when she returned from these people; for I knew all her affairs, and, through her, all their affairs; and I took an interest in whatever concerned her or hers.

One Sunday evening, after she had been spending the afternoon with this family, observing that she was unusually silent, I said to her while she was undressing me,

"Well, Françoise, haven't you anything to tell me? How are your friends? Has Madame Pelletier got rid of her grippe?"

Françoise started as if I had awakened her out of a reverie, and said, "*Oh! Oui, Madame; oui, mercie; elle se porte bien aujourd'hui.*"

"And Monsieur Pelletier and the children, are they well?"

"*Oui, Madame, mercie; ils se porte bien.*"

These curt answers were so unlike those she generally gave me, that I was sure her mind was pre-occupied, and that something had happened since we parted in the morning; so I turned round to look her in the face, saying, "*Mais, qu'avez-vous done, Françoise? Qu'est-ce qu'il y a?*"

Then I saw what I had not observed before, that she was very pale, and that her cheeks had a glazed look, which showed that she had been crying.

"*Mais, ma bonne Françoise,*" I said; "*vous avez quelque chose—est-il arrive quelque malheur a Metz?*"

"*C'est çela, Madame,*" answered Françoise, who had a brother there whom she had not seen for several years, but to whom she still continued affectionately attached. His name was Benoît, and he was in a good service as *garde forestier* to a nobleman, who possessed very extensive estates, "*près de chez nous,*" as Françoise said. He had a wife and children; and some time before the period I am referring to, Françoise had told me with great satisfaction, that in order to make him more comfortable, the Prince de

M—— had given Benoît the privilege of gathering up all the dead wood in the forest to sell for firewood, which, as the estate was very large, rendered his situation extremely profitable. When she said, "*C'est çela, Madame*," Françoise, who had just encased me in my dressing-gown, sunk into a chair, and having declared that she was "*bête, très bête*," she gave way to a hearty good cry, after which, being somewhat relieved, she told me the following strange story.

"You remember," she said, "that the Prince was so good as to give Benoît all the dead wood of the forest and a great thing it was for him and his family, as you will think, when I tell you it was upwards of two thousand francs a year to him. In short, he was growing rich, and perhaps he was getting to think too much of his money and too little of the "*bon Dieu*"—at all events, this privilege which the Prince gave him to make him comfortable, and which made him a great man among the foresters, has been the cause of a dreadful calamity."

"How?" said I.

"We never heard anything of what had happened," said she, "till yesterday, when Monsieur Pelletier received a letter from Benoît's wife, and another from a cousin of ours, relating what I am going to tell you, and saying that both he and his family had wished to keep it secret, but that it was no longer possible."

"Well, and what has happened?"

"*La chose la plus incroyable! Eh, bien, Madame*, it appears that one day last autumn, Benoît went out in the forest to gather the dead wood. He had his cart with him, and as he gathered it he bound it into faggots and threw it in the cart.

"He had extended his search this day to a remote part of the forest, and found himself in a spot he did not remember to have visited before; indeed, it was evident to him that he had not, or he could not have escaped seeing an old wooden cross which was lying on the ground, and had apparently fallen into that recumbent position from old age. It was such a cross as is usually set up where a life has been lost, whether by murder or by suicide; or sometimes when poor wanderers are frozen to death or lost in the deep winter snows. He looked about for the grave, but saw no indication of one; and he tried to remember if any catastrophe had happened there in his time, but could recall none. He took up the cross and examined it. He saw that the wood was decayed, and it bore such marks of antiquity, that he had no doubt the person whose grave it had marked had died before he was born—it looked as if it might be a hundred years old.

"*Eh, bien*," said Françoise, wiping her eyes, into which the tears kept starting, "of course you will think that Benoît, or anybody in the world who had the fear of God before his eyes, as he could not find the grave to replace it as it should be, would have laid it reverently down where he had found it, saying a prayer for the soul of the deceased; but alas! the demon of avarice tempted him, and he had not the heart to forego that poor cross, but bound it up into a faggot with the rest of the dead wood he found there, and threw it into his cart!"

"Well, Françoise," said I, "you know I am not a Catholic, but I respect the custom of erecting these crosses, and I do think your brother was very wrong; I suppose he has lost the Prince's favour by such impious greediness."

"*Pire que ça!* worse than that," she replied. "It appears that while he was committing this wicked action, he felt an extraordinary chill come over him, which made him think that, though it had been a mild day, the evening must have suddenly turned very cold, and hastily throwing the faggot into his cart, he directed his steps homeward. But, walk as he would, he still felt this chill down his back, so that he turned his head to look where the wind blew from, when he saw, with some dismay, a mysterious-looking figure following close upon his footsteps. It moved noiselessly on, and was covered with a sort of black mantle that prevented his discerning the features. Not liking its appearance, he jumped into the cart, and drove home as fast as he could, without looking behind him; and when he got into his own farmyard he felt quite relieved, particularly, as, when he alighted, he saw no more of this unpleasant-looking stranger. So he began unloading his cart, taking out the faggots, one by one, and throwing them upon the ground; but when he threw down the one that contained the cross, he received a blow upon his face, so sharp that it made him stagger, and involuntarily shout aloud. His wife and children were close by, but there was no one else to be seen; and they would have disbelieved him and fancied he had accidentally hit himself with the faggot, but that they saw the distinct mark on his cheek of a blow given with an open hand. However, he went into supper, perplexed and uncomfortable; but when he went to bed this fearful phantom stood by his side, silent and terrible, visible to him, but invisible to others. In short, Madame, this awful figure haunted him, till, in spite of his shame, he resolved to consult our cousin Jerome about it.

"But Jerome laughed, and said it was all fancy and superstition. 'You got frightened at having brought away this poor devil's cross, and then you fancy he's haunting you,' said he.

"But Benoît declared that he had thought nothing about the cross, except that it would make firewood, and that he had no more believed in ghosts than Jerome. 'But now,' said he, 'something must be done. I can get no sleep, and am losing my health; if you can't help me, I must go to the priest and consult him.'

"'Why don't you take back the cross and put it where you found it?' said Jerome.

"'Because I am afraid to touch it, and dare not go to that part of the forest.'

"So Jerome, who did not believe a word about the ghost, offered to go with him and replace the cross. Benoît gladly accepted, more especially as he said he saw the apparition standing even then beside him, apparently listening to the conversation. Jerome laughed at the idea; however, Benoît lifted the cross reverently into the cart and away they went into the forest. When they reached the spot, Benoît pointed out the tree under which he had found it; and as he was shaking and trembling, Jerome took up the cross and laid it on the ground; but as he did so, he received a violent blow from an invisible hand, and at the same moment saw Benoît fall to the ground. He thought he had been struck too, but it afterwards appeared that he had fainted from having seen the phantom with its upraised hand striking his cousin. However, they left the cross and came away; but there was an end to Jerome's laughter, and he was afraid the apparition would now haunt him. Nothing of the sort happened; but poor Benoît's health had been so shaken by this frightful occurrence that he cannot get the better of it; his friends have advised change of scene, and he is coming to Paris next week."

This was the story Françoise told me, and in a few days I heard that he had arrived, and was staying with Monsieur Pelletier; but the shock had been too great for his nerves, and he died shortly after. They assured me that, previous to that fatal expedition into the forest, he had been a hale, hearty man, totally exempt from superstitious fancies of any sort; and, in short, wholly devoted to advancing his worldly prosperity and getting money.

A DREAM OF DEATH

HER EYES WERE SMARTING from long want of sleep. Her head swam, and she felt a sudden faintness. Involuntarily she groped for support. Faint and deadly sleepy, she let her arms fall down on the table and her face on her clasped hands.

There were strange sounds around her, heavy sighs and a monotonous soughing mingling with the rustling of faded leaves. She wanted to lift her head to see what it was, but could not raise it, however much she tried. At last she succeeded. What is this? she thought. Everything seemed to loom so large round her, and the ceiling seemed so high up, and the light was pale grey, like that of a distant and misty moon, and there, along the wall, stood rows of beds with white sheets and blankets tucked in tightly, and beneath the blankets lay human beings, stiffly stretched out, and groaning. Now and then they raised their heads and prayed with heart-rending voices that their tight coverings might be loosened. But no one answered. By the side of the high narrow door opposite stood a figure with bound hands in a long white shining robe, fastened to the wall by a thick dark rope which was twisted round the waist. The eyes were wide open and had no pupils, but the whites were large and protruding, and out of the mouth hung a long tongue, black as pitch. Else wanted to rise, but she could not move a limb. Stiff with fear, she stared at the door. In a few bounds she would be able to reach it. But supposing it was locked now and the key were gone. Yes, it was locked, and there was no key: she saw that distinctly. She then felt herself become like a paralysed mass, and she began to glide down from the chair. But just at that moment the door opened noiselessly and four men entered quietly, carrying with them a long light coffin, curved into a semi-circle up at the top. The opening of the upper half was covered in front with a pane of glass, and through this Else saw a human head lying sideways with an emaciated, lifeless face, the colour of which seemed black as lead against the white pillow. In a moment she knew it was herself and that she was dead. Struggling to make some sound, she gave a shriek, fell face downwards on the floor, and woke up.

THE MYSTERIOUS
HORSEMAN

O NE SUMMER DAY, at the commencement of the
present century, I was travelling from Bala in
Merionethshire to Machynlleth, in the neighbouring county
of Montgomery, in order to attend a religious meeting. I left
Bala about 2 p.m., and travelled on horseback, and alone.
My journey lay through a wild, desolate part of the country,
and one which, at that time, was almost uninhabited.
When I had performed about half my journey, as I was
emerging from a wood situated at the commencement of a
long steep decline, I observed, coming towards me, a man
on foot. By his appearance, judging from the sickle which
he carried sheathed in straw over his shoulder, he was
doubtless a reaper in search of employment. As he drew
near, I recognised a man whom I had seen at the door of
the village inn of Llanwhellyn, where I had stopped to bait
my horse. On our meeting, he touched his hat and asked if
I could tell him the time of day. I pulled out my watch for
the purpose, noticing at the same time the peculiar look

which the man cast at its heavy silver case. Nothing else, however, occurred to excite any suspicion on my part, so, wishing him a "good afternoon," I continued my journey.

When I had ridden about half-way down the hill I noticed something moving, and in the same direction as myself, on the other side of a large hedge, which ran nearly parallel with the road, and ultimately terminated at a gate through which I had to pass. At first I thought it an animal of some kind or other, but soon discovered, by certain depressions in the hedge, that it was a man running in a stooping position. I continued for a short time to watch his progress with some curiosity, but my curiosity soon changed to fear when I recognised the reaper with whom I had conversed a few minutes before, engaged in tearing off the straw-band which sheathed his sickle.

He hurried on until he reached the gate, and then concealed himself behind the hedge within a few yards of the road. I did not then doubt for a moment that he had resolved to attack—perhaps murder—me for the sake of my watch and whatever money I might have about me. I looked around in all directions, but not a single human being was to be seen, so reining in my horse I asked myself in much alarm what I could do. Should I turn back? no; my business was of the utmost importance to the cause for which I was journeying, and as long as there existed the faintest possibility of getting there, I could not think of returning.

Should I trust to the speed of my horse, and endeavour to dash by the man at full speed? No; for the gate through which I had to pass was not open. Could I leave the road and make my way through the fields? I could not, for I was hemmed in by rocky banks, or high hedges on both sides. The idea of risking a personal encounter could not be entertained for a moment, for what chance could I, weak and unarmed, have against a powerful man with a dangerous weapon in his hand? What course, then, should I pursue? I could not tell; and at length, in despair, rather than in a spirit of humble trust and confidence, I bowed my head and offered up a silent prayer. This had a soothing effect upon my mind, so that, refreshed and invigorated, I proceeded anew to consider the difficulties of my position.

At this juncture, my horse, growing impatient at the delay, started off. I clutched the reins, which I had let fall on his neck, for the purpose of checking him, when happening to turn my eyes, I saw to my utter astonishment that I was no longer alone. There, by my side, I beheld a horseman in a dark dress, mounted on a white steed. In intense amazement I gazed upon him: where could he have come from? He appeared as suddenly as if he had sprung from the earth. He must have been riding behind and have overtaken me. And yet, I had not heard the slightest sound; it was mysterious, inexplicable. But the joy of being released from my perilous position soon overcame my feelings of wonder, and I began at once to address my companion. I asked him if he had seen any one, and then described to him what had taken place, and how relieved I felt by his sudden appearance, which now removed all cause of fear. He made no reply, and on looking at his face, he seemed paying but slight attention to my words, but continued intently gazing in the direction of the gate, now about a quarter of a mile ahead. I followed his gaze, and saw the reaper emerge from his concealment and cut across a field to our left, re-sheathing his sickle as he hurried along. He had evidently seen that I was no longer alone, and had relinquished his intended attempt.

All cause for alarm being gone, I once more sought to enter into conversation with my deliverer, but again without the slightest success. Not a word did he deign to give me in reply. I continued talking, however, as we rode on our way towards the gate, though I confess feeling both surprised and hurt at my companion's mysterious silence. Once, however, and only once, did I hear his voice. Having watched the figure of the reaper disappear over the brow of a neighbouring hill, I turned to my companion and said, "Can it for a moment be doubted that my prayer was heard, and that you were sent for my deliverance by the Lord?" Then it was that I thought I heard the horseman speak, and that he uttered the single word, "Amen." Not another word did he give utterance to, though I tried to elicit from him replies to my questions, both in English and Welsh.

We were now approaching the gate, which I hastened to open, and having done so with my stick, I waited at the side of the road for him to pass through; but he came not; I turned my head to look—the mysterious horseman was gone! I was dumbfounded; I looked back in the direction from which we had just been riding, but though I could command a view of the road for a considerable distance, he was not to be seen. He had disappeared as mysteriously as he had come. What could have become of him? He could not have gone through the gate, nor have made his horse leap the high hedges which on both sides shut in the road. Where was he? Had I been dreaming? Was it an apparition, a spectre which had been riding by my side for the last ten minutes? Could it be possible that I had seen no man or horse at all, and that the vision was but a creature of my imagination? I tried hard to convince myself that this was the case, but in vain: for, unless someone had been with me, why had the reaper re-sheathed his murderous-looking sickle and fled? Surely no; this mysterious horseman was no creation of my brain. I had seen him. Who could he have been?

I asked myself this question again and again; and then a feeling of profound awe began to creep over my soul. I remembered the singular way of his first appearance—his

166

long silence—and then again the single word to which he had given utterance; I called to mind that this reply had been elicited from him by my mentioning the name of the Lord, and that this was the single occasion on which I had done so. What could I then believe? But one thing, and that was, that my prayer had indeed been heard, and that help had been given from on high at a time of great danger. Full of this thought, I dismounted, and throwing myself on my knees, I offered up a prayer of thankfulness to Him who had heard my cry, and found help for me in time of need.

I then mounted my horse and continued my journey. But through the long years that have elapsed since that memorable summer's day, I have never for a moment wavered in my belief that, in the mysterious horseman, I had a special interference of Providence, by which means I was delivered from a position of extreme danger.

THE BLIND BEGGAR
OF ODESA

A N OLD BLIND MAN of Odesa, named Michel, had, for many years, been accustomed to get his living by seating himself every morning on a beam in one of the timber yards, with a wooden bowl at his feet, into which the passengers cast their alms. This long-continued practice had made him well known to the inhabitants, and as he was believed to have been formerly a soldier, his blindness was attributed to the numerous wounds he had received in battle. For his own part he spoke little, and never contradicted this opinion.

One night Michel, by some accident, fell in with a little girl of ten years old, named Powleska, who was friendless and on the verge of perishing with cold and hunger. The old man took her home, and adopted her, and from that time, instead of sitting in the timber yards, he went about the streets in her company, asking alms at the doors of the houses. The child called him father, and they were extremely happy together. But when they had pursued their mode of life for about five years a misfortune befell them. A theft having been committed in a house which they had visited in the morning, Powleska was suspected and arrested, and the blind man was left once more alone. But, instead of resuming his former habits, he now disappeared altogether, and this circumstance causing the suspicion to extend to him, the girl was brought before the magistrate to be interrogated with regard to his probable place of concealment.

"Do you know where Michel is?" inquired the magistrate.

"He is dead," replied she, shedding a torrent of tears.

As the girl had been shut up for three days, without any means of obtaining information from without, this answer, together with her unfeigned distress, naturally excited considerable surprise.

"Who told you he was dead?" they inquired.

"Nobody!"

"Then how can you know it?"

"I saw him killed!"

"But you have not been out of the prison?"

"But I saw it, nevertheless!"

"But how was that possible? Explain what you mean!"

"I cannot. All I can say is that I saw him killed."

"When was he killed, and how?"

"It was the night I was arrested."

"That cannot be; he was alive when you were seized."

"Yes, he was; he was killed an hour after that. They stabbed him with a knife."

"Where were you then?"

"I can't tell; but I saw it."

The confidence with which the girl asserted what seemed to her hearers impossible and absurd, disposed them to imagine that she was either really insane or pretending to be so; so, leaving Michel aside, they proceeded to interrogate her about the robbery, asking her if she was guilty.

"Oh no!" she answered.

"Then how came the property to be found about you?"

"I don't know; I saw nothing but the murder."

"But there are no grounds for supposing Michel is dead; his body has not been found."

"It is in the aqueduct."

"And do you know who slew him?"

"Yes, it is a woman. Michel was walking very slowly after I was taken from him. A woman came behind him with a large kitchen knife; but he heard her, and turned round; and then the woman flung a piece of grey stuff over his head, and struck him repeatedly with the knife; the grey stuff was much stained with the blood. Michel fell at the eighth blow, and the woman dragged the body to the aqueduct and let it fall in without ever lifting the stuff which stuck to his face."

As it was easy to verify these latter assertions, they despatched people to the spot; and there the body was found with the piece of stuff over his head, exactly as she had described. But when they asked her how she knew all this, she could only answer, "I don't know."

"But you know who killed him?"

"Not exactly; it is the same woman that put out his eyes; but, perhaps, he will tell me her name to-night; and if he does, I will tell it to you."

"Who do you mean by he?"

"Why, Michel, to be sure!"

During the whole of the following night, without allowing her to suspect their intention, they watched her; and it was observed that she never lay down, but sat upon the bed in a sort of lethargic slumber. Her body was quite motionless, except at intervals, when this repose was interrupted by violent nervous shocks, which pervaded her whole frame. On the ensuing day, the moment she was brought before the judge, she declared that she was now able to tell them the name of the assassin.

"But stay," said the magistrate; "did Michel never tell you, when he was alive, how he lost his sight?"

"No; but the morning before I was arrested, he promised me to do so; and that was the cause of his death."

"How could that be?"

"Last night Michel came to me, and he pointed to the

man hidden behind the scaffolding on which he and I had been sitting. He showed me the man listening to us, when he said, 'I'll tell you all about that tonight'; and then the man—"

"Do you know the name of this man?"

"It is Luck. He went afterwards to a broad street that leads down to the harbour, and he entered the third house on the right—"

"What is the name of the street?"

"I don't know; but the house is one storey lower than the adjoining ones. Luck told Catherine what he had heard, and she proposed to him to assassinate Michel; but he refused, saying, 'It is bad enough to have burnt out his eyes fifteen years before, whilst he was asleep at your door, and to have kidnapped him into the country.'

Then I went in to ask charity, and Catherine put a piece of plate into my pocket, that I might be arrested: then she hid herself behind the aqueduct to wait for Michel, and she killed him."

"But, since you say all this, why did you keep the plate—why didn't you give him information?"

"But I didn't see it then. Michel showed it me last night."

"But what should induce Catherine to do this?"

"Michel was her husband, and she had forsaken him to come to Odesa and marry again. One night, fifteen years ago, she saw Michel, who had come to seek her. She slipped hastily into her house, and Michel, who thought she had not seen him, lay down at her door to watch; but he fell asleep, and then Luck burned out his eyes, and carried him to a distance."

"And is it Michel who has told you this?"

"Yes: he came, very pale and covered with blood; and he took me by the hand and showed me all this with his fingers."

Upon this, Luck and Catherine were arrested; and it was ascertained that she had actually been married to Michel in the year 1819, at Rherson. They at first denied the accusation, but Powleska insisted, and they subsequently confessed the crime. When they communicated the circumstances of the confession to Powleska, she said, "I was told it last night."

THE STORY OF
MAJOR WEIR

I T MUST HAVE BEEN a sad scandal to this peculiar com-
munity [*the "Bowhead Saints"*] when Major Weir, one
of their number, was found to have been so wretched an
example of human infirmity. The house occupied by this
man still exists, though in an altered shape, in a little court
accessible by a narrow passage near the first angle of the
street. His history is obscurely reported; but it appears that
he was of a good family in Lanarkshire, and had been one
of the ten thousand men sent by the Scottish Covenanting
Estates in 1641 to assist in suppressing the Irish Papists.
He became distinguished for a life of peculiar sanctity,
even in an age when that was the prevailing tone of the
public mind. According to a contemporary account: "His
garb was still a cloak, and somewhat dark, and he never
went without his staff. He was a tall man, and ordinarily
looked down to the ground; a grim countenance, and a big
nose. At length he became so notoriously regarded among

the Presbyterian strict sect, that if four met together, be sure Major Weir was one. At private meetings he prayed to admiration, which made many of that stamp court his converse. He never married, but lived in a private lodging with his sister, Grizel Weir. Many resorted to his house, to join with him, and hear him pray; but it was observed that he could not officiate in any holy duty without the black staff, or rod, in his hand, and leaning upon it, which made those who heard him pray admire his flood in prayer, his ready extemporary expression, his heavenly gesture; so that he was thought more angel than man, and was termed by some of the holy sisters ordinarily 'Angelical Thomas.'" Plebeian imaginations have since fructified regarding the staff, and crones will still seriously tell how it could run a message to a shop for any article which its proprietor wanted; how it could answer the door when any one called upon its master; and that it used to be often seen running before him, in the capacity of a link-boy, as he walked down the Lawnmarket.

After a life characterised externally by all the graces of devotion, but polluted in secret by crimes of the most revolting nature, and which little needed the addition of wizardry to excite the horror of living men, Major Weir fell into a severe sickness, which affected his mind so much, that he made an open and voluntary confession of all his wickedness. The tale was at first so incredible, that the provost, Sir Andrew Ramsay, refused for some time to take him into custody. At length himself, his sister (partner of one of his crimes), and his staff, were secured by the magistrates, together with certain sums of money, which were found wrapped up in rags in different parts of the house. One of these pieces of rag being thrown into the fire by a bailie who had taken the whole in charge, flew up the chimney, and made an explosion like a cannon. While the wretched man lay in prison, he made no scruple to disclose the particulars of his guilt, but refused to address himself to the Almighty for pardon. To every request that he would pray, he answered in screams: "Torment me no more—I am tormented enough already!" Even the offer of a Presbyterian clergyman, instead of an established Episcopal minister of the city, had no effect upon him. He was tried April 9, 1670, and being found guilty, was sentenced to be strangled and burnt between Edinburgh and Leith. His sister, who was tried at the same time, was sentenced to be hanged in the Grassmarket. The execution of the profligate Major took place, April 14, at the place indicated by the judge. When the rope was about his neck, to prepare him for the fire, he was bid to say: "Lord, be merciful to me!" but he answered, as before: "Let me alone—I will not—I have lived as a beast, and I must die as a beast!" After he had dropped lifeless in the flames, his stick was also cast into the fire; and, "whatever incantation was in it," says the contemporary writer already quoted,* "the persons present own that it gave rare turnings, and was long a-burning, as also himself."

The conclusion to which the humanity of the present age would come regarding Weir—that he was mad—is favoured by some circumstances; for instance, his answering one who asked if he had ever seen the devil, that "the only feeling he ever had of him was in the dark." What chiefly countenances the idea, is the unequivocal lunacy of the sister. This miserable woman confessed to witchcraft, and related, in a serious manner, many things which could not be true. Many years before, a fiery coach, she said, had come to her brother's door in broad day, and a stranger invited them to enter, and they proceeded to Dalkeith. On the way, another person came and whispered in her brother's ear something which affected him; it proved to be supernatural intelligence of the defeat of the Scotch army at Worcester, which took place that day. Her brother's power, she said, lay in his staff. She also had a gift for spinning above other women, but the yarn broke to pieces in the loom. Her mother, she declared, had been also a witch. "The secretest thing that I, or any of the family could do, when once a mark appeared upon her brow, she could tell it them, though done at a great distance." This mark could

* The Rev. Mr Frazer, minister of Wardlaw, in his "Divine Providences" (MS. Adv. Lib.), dated 1670.

also appear on her own forehead when she pleased. At the request of the company present, "she put back her head-dress, and seeming to frown, there was an exact horseshoe shaped for nails in her wrinkles, terrible enough, I assure you, to the stoutest beholder."* At the place of execution she acted in a furious manner, and with difficulty could be prevented from throwing off her clothes, in order to die, as she said, "with all the shame she could."

The treatise just quoted makes it plain that the case of Weir and his sister had immediately become a fruitful theme for the imaginations of the vulgar. We there receive the following story:—"Some few days before he discovered himself, a gentlewoman coming from the Castle-hill, where her husband's niece was lying-in of a child, about midnight perceived about the Bowhead three women in windows, shouting, laughing, and clapping their hands. The gentlewoman went forward, till, at Major Weir's door, there arose, as from the street, a woman about the length of two ordinary females, and stepped forward. The gentle-woman, not as yet excessively feared, bid her maid step on, if by the lantern they could see what she was; but haste what they could, this long-legged spectre was still before them, moving her body with a vehement cachinnation and great immeasurable laughter. At this rate the two strove for place, till the giantess came to a narrow lane in the

* "Satan's Invisible World Discovered."

179

Bow, commonly called the Stinking Close, into which she turning, and the gentlewoman looking after her, perceived the close full of flaming torches (she could give them no other name), and as if it had been a great number of people stentoriously laughing, and gaping with tahees of laughter. This sight, at so dead a time of night, no people being in the windows belonging to the close, made her and her servant haste home, declaring all that they saw to the rest of the family."

For upwards of a century after Major Weir's death, he continued to be the bugbear of the Bow, and his house remained uninhabited. His apparition was frequently seen at night, flitting, like a black and silent shadow, about the street. His house, though known to be deserted by everything human, was sometimes observed at midnight to be full of lights, and heard to emit strange sounds, as of dancing, howling, and, what is strangest of all, spinning. Some people occasionally saw the Major issue from the low close at midnight, mounted on a black horse without a head, and gallop off in a whirlwind of flame. Nay, sometimes the whole of the inhabitants of the Bow would be roused from their sleep at an early hour in the morning by the sound as of a coach and six, first rattling up the Lawnmarket, and then thundering down the Bow, stopping at the head of the terrible close for a few minutes, and then rattling and thundering back again—being neither more

nor less than Satan come in one of his best equipages to take home the Major and his sister, after they had spent a night's leave of absence in their terrestrial dwelling.

About fifty years ago, when the shades of superstition began universally to give way in Scotland, Major Weir's house came to be regarded with less terror by the neighbours, and an attempt was made by the proprietor to find a person who should be bold enough to inhabit it. Such a person was procured in William Patullo, a poor man of dissipated habits, who, having been at one time a soldier and a traveller, had come to disregard in a great measure the superstitions of his native country, and was now glad to possess a house upon the low terms offered by the landlord, at whatever risk. Upon its being known that Major Weir's house was about to be re-inhabited, a great deal of curiosity was felt by people of all ranks as to the result of the experiment; for there was scarcely a native of the city who had not felt, since his boyhood, an intense interest in all that concerned that awful fabric, and yet remembered the numerous terrible stories which he had heard respecting it. Even before entering upon his hazardous undertaking, William Patullo was looked upon with a flattering sort of interest, similar to that which we feel respecting a regiment on the march to active conflict. It was the hope of many that he would be the means of retrieving a valuable possession from the dominion of darkness. But Satan soon let them know that he does not tamely relinquish any of the outposts of his kingdom.

On the very first night after Patullo and his spouse had taken up their abode in the house, as the worthy couple were lying awake in their bed, not unconscious of a certain degree of fear—a dim uncertain light proceeding from the gathered embers of their fire, and all being silent around them—they suddenly saw a form like that of a calf, which came forward to the bed, and, setting its fore-feet upon the stock, looked steadfastly at the unfortunate pair. When it had contemplated them thus for a few minutes, to their great relief it at length took itself away, and, slowly retiring, gradually vanished from their sight. As might be expected, they deserted the house next morning; and for another half-century no other attempt was made to embank this part of the world of light from the aggressions of the world of darkness.

It may here be mentioned that, at no very remote time, there were several houses in the Old Town which had the credit of being haunted. It is said there is one at this day in the Lawnmarket (a flat), which has been shut up from time immemorial. The story goes that one night, as preparations were making for a supper-party, something occurred which obliged the family, as well as all the assembled guests, to retire with precipitation, and lock up the house. From that night it has never once been opened, nor was any of the furniture withdrawn: the very goose which was undergoing the process of being roasted at the time of the occurrence, is still at the fire! No one knows to whom the house belongs; no one ever inquires after it; no one living ever saw the inside of it; it is a condemned house! There is something peculiarly dreadful about a house under these circumstances. What sights of horror might present themselves if it were entered! Satan is the *ultimus haeres* of all such unclaimed property!

MARSHAL BLÜCHER

I N THE AUTUMN of the year in which Waterloo had been fought, Marshal Blücher quitted France for the last time. Chagrined at finding himself reduced to a life of inaction, he retired to his property, and fell into a state of melancholy, increased by an attack of dropsy on the chest. From this time a change came over his character; the rough and ready soldier became timid, and even nervous. He would not remain in the dark; solitude was agonising, and such was the uneasiness caused by his failing health, that the King of Prussia (father of the present Emperor of Germany) started for Krieblowitz as soon as he learned that his old and favourite general had several times expressed a wish to see him before dying. The king arrived in the evening at the castle, and was instantly conducted to Blücher, then in his seventy-fourth year.

On seeing the king, Marshal Blücher tried to rise for the purpose of receiving His Majesty, who kindly prevented him, and sat down by his side; when the old soldier, after dismissing his attendants, spoke as follows:—

"Sire, I entreated you to come here, as I heard you were in the neighbourhood, yet had you been at the other extremity of Europe, dying as I am now, I must have endeavoured to have reached you, for I have a terrible secret to reveal. Sire, be pleased to look at me well, and assure yourself that I am now in the full enjoyment of my reason, and that I am not mad; for at times I almost think I am deluded into mistaking recollections of past events for visions of the present war. But no, I cannot doubt! It must be true.

"When, Sire, in 1876, the Seven Years' War broke out, my father who lived on his estate of Gross Renson, sent me to one of our relations, the Princess Krauswick, in the Isle of Rugen. I was then fourteen, and after a time passed in the old fortress without news from my family, I entered a regiment of hussars in the Swedish service, and being taken prisoner at Suokow, the Prussian Government pressed me to take service in its army. For a year I resisted, and only obtained my liberty by accepting the rank of cornet in the regiment of Black Hussars. I then obtained leave for some months, as I was very anxious concerning my mother and sisters, and started at once for Gross Renson, which had been the scene of war during my year's imprisonment.

"It is just fifty-nine years ago, this very day, the 12th August (1816), and about the same hour I am speaking to your majesty, verging toward midnight, when in the midst of a raging storm, and after long wandering in the forest, I reached my father's house, drenched to the skin and alone, for my servant, bewildered by the tempest, had lost me in the darkness of the night. Without dismounting, I struck the nail-studded oaken door with the butt end of my whip. No one replied, though I hammered again and again at the door; until, losing all patience, I jumped off my horse, when the door appeared to open of its own accord, as I could perceive no one, and I entered; and hurrying up the steps, quickly penetrated the interior.

"There was no light to be seen or sound heard. I confess that my heart sank within me, and a cold shudder ran through my veins. 'What folly!' I exclaimed; 'the house must be empty; my family must have left when I quitted it, and have not returned, still I must remain for the night.' I reached my father's bedroom; a faint and fitful flame threw a dim light upon a group of persons seated, amongst whom I recognised my father, mother, and four sisters, who rose on seeing me enter. I was about to throw myself into my father's arms, when he arrested me by a solemn gesture. I held out my arms to my mother, but she retreated with a mournful air. I called out to my sisters, who, taking each other by the hand, again seated themselves.

"'Do you not know me?' I cried. 'Is it thus you receive me after so long a separation? Do you not know that I am now serving Prussia? I was compelled to make the sacrifice in order to regain my liberty, and to see you. But no one responds to my affection. My mother, you are silent! My sisters, have you forgotten the love of our childhood, and the games of which these walls have been the silent witnesses?'

"At these last words my sisters seemed to be moved, and they spoke to one another in a low voice: they rose up and signalled to me to approach. One of them then knelt down before my mother, and hid her face in her lap, as if she wished to play at a game called 'Hot-kok-hiry' (a childish game, where one has his eyes bound, and guesses who strikes with the flat of the hand). Surprised at this strange freak at such a solemn time, I nevertheless touched my sister's hand with the whip that I still grasped, as a mysterious force seemed to impel me so to do. Then came my turn to kneel before my mother, and to hide my face in her lap.

"Oh, horror! I felt through her silk dress a cold angular form; I heard a sound of rattling bones; and when a hand was placed in mine, the hand remained there; and it was the hand of a skeleton! I arose with a cry of terror; all had disappeared, and there only remained to me of this dreadful vision the human remains which I convulsively grasped.

"Almost beside myself, I ran from the chamber, hurried downstairs, jumped on my horse, and galloped wildly through the forest. At daybreak my horse sank beneath me and expired. I fell insensible at the foot of a large tree, and was found there by my attendants with my skull fractured. I almost died from the combined effects of horror of mind and the injury in my head, and it was only after some weeks of fever and delirium that I regained my senses, and gradually recovered.

"It was then I learned that all my family had perished in the terrible war which had desolated Mecklenburg, and that my father's castle had been several times pillaged and sacked. Scarcely convalescent, I hastened to the castle to render the last rites to my deceased parents and sisters; but after a most rigorous search no trace of their remains could be found, save one hand only—a female hand, surrounded by a golden bracelet, lay on the floor of the room in which the fatal apparition had appeared to me. I took the golden chain—the same, your majesty, which I now hold in my hands—and deposited the hand, all that remained of my family, in the oratory chapel.

"Many years have glided by since that awful scene which I witnessed in my father's castle; and it was only two months ago, while lying in this arm-chair, a slight noise awoke me. I looked up. There stood my father, mother, and four sisters around, just as they appeared on that awful night at the castle of Gross Renson. My sisters commenced playing at the same game, and signalled me to advance. 'Never! never!' I exclaimed; and then the apparitions, joining hands, passed slowly around my chair. 'Justice!' cried my father, as he passed before me; 'Penitence!' exclaimed my mother, leaning towards me; 'Prayer!' murmured my youngest sister; 'The sword!' sighed another; 'The 12th of August, at midnight!' whispered the eldest. Again the procession moved slowly around me thrice; then, with one terrible roar, they all cried out together, 'Adieu! adieu! to our next meeting!'

"I felt then it was a warning of my approaching death, and that I had only to look to God to receive my soul, and bid farewell to your majesty and friends."

"My dear Marshall" said the king, "what you have related to me is very strange; still, do you not think the vision may have been caused by delirium? Take courage, strive against these hallucinations, and you will rally and live many years yet. Will you not try and believe what I say? Give me your hand."

The king, receiving no answer, took the old man's hand. It was icy cold. Just then the old clock on the mantelpiece struck the midnight hour. The spirit of Marshal Blücher had quietly passed away.

SIR HULDBRAND'S WIFE

Undine is a beautiful maiden whose parentage is wrapped in mystery. She has been reared and cherished by a kind old couple before whose door she was found lying, a helpless waif, in her infancy. She dwells with these on a small peninsula amid the streams of a lonely forest.

At length a knight, Sir Huldbrand, is driven by a storm to seek refuge with Undine's foster-parents. He is hospitably entertained, and falls in love with Undine. They are united by a holy father who has also sought an asylum in the cottage. The day after the wedding, Undine asks her husband to carry her across to an islet, and there gives the following account of herself.

"YOU MUST KNOW, my loved lord, that there are beings in the elements that bear great resemblance to you, and yet but rarely appear before you. Wondrous salamanders play and glitter in the flames; meagre malicious gnomes dwell in the recesses of the earth; the sylphs inhabit the air, and dwell in the hidden shades of the dark grove; and water-spirits—an extensive race—are dispersed in the rivers, brooks, lakes, and oceans. Delightful is it to dwell in resounding arbours of crystal, to which the sun, the moon, and the stars convey the glorious light of heaven; under the umbrage of lofty trees of coral, bearing fruit of the most beautiful blue and red colour, which grow in those gardens; or to roam on the pure sand of the ocean, over beautiful shells, and to contemplate things grand and beautiful, which the ancient world possessed, and which the present is no longer worthy to enjoy—lofty and stately monuments that the floods have covered with their veil of silver, and bedewed with limpid waters, extracting from them moss-flowers and tufted reeds. Those that dwell there are benign and fair, mostly fairer than human beings. They that ply upon the water have frequently been so fortunate as to surprise some beauteous inhabitant of those regions when such a one rose above the wave and filled the air with the charming sound of her voice; and those men have been lavish in their reports. The inhabitants of those fair regions are known by the name of Undines, and you, my honoured lord, are now beholding a real Undine."

The knight would have persuaded himself his lovely wife was again indulging in one of her frolicsome humours, and that she took pleasure in bantering him with some singular and fanciful tale. Yet, strongly as he endeavoured to believe this, he found his effort unsuccessful. A thrilling emotion pervaded him, and, unable to utter a word, he continued to gaze, full of wonder and with unaverted eye, on the fair

narrator. She, full of dejection, shook her head, heaved a deep sigh, and continued as follows:—

"We should be better off than you other human beings—for human beings we call ourselves, as indeed, in our outward appearance and shape, we are; but one great evil is coupled with our lot. We, and those of our kin in other elements, pass away and moulder into dust—the spirit as well as the body—so that not a vestige of us remains; and when you awake to a purer life, we shall have passed away as the waving flame, or the wind and the billow of the deep. This is because we are not endowed with a soul. The element that moves us, and frequently obeys us while we live always scatters our dust when we die, and we are thoughtlessly gay, like the nightingale, the goldfish, and other happy and beautiful creatures in Nature.

"But all strive to rise higher in their scale of being. Thus, my father, who is a potent prince of the waters in the Mediterranean, desired that his only daughter should imbibe a soul, even if it should fall to her lot to have her share of the afflictions that are incident to those so highly blessed. But a soul can be obtained by one of our race only by means of being intimately connected by the bands of love with a mortal. I have gained it, and to you, my most honoured and beloved lord, I am indebted for the inestimable benefit; and I shall remain indebted to you, even if you make me wretched for the rest of my life. Alas! what would be my hapless condition, were you to shun and spurn me? Yet, by duplicity, I do not wish to hold you. If, then, it be your intention to reject me, do it now, and return alone to the other bank. I shall plunge into this brook, who is my uncle, and who, like an anchorite, delights in dwelling here in this forest, separated from his other relatives. But he is powerful, and dear to many great streams; and as he conducted me, a young and smiling child, to yonder cottage, so he will re-conduct me hence to my parents, an affectionate and enduring wife, endowed with an immortal soul."

She would have said more, but Huldbrand embraced her with the tenderest emotion, and bore her back to the other bank. Then, first, amid tears and a thousand kisses, he swore that he would never forsake her, and accounted himself happier in possessing her than Pygmalion, the Grecian sculptor, when Venus, in pity, animated the fair damsel that himself had cut out of the stone. In unbounded trust Undine leaned on his arm, and wandered back to the cottage, feeling how little occasion she had to regret the crystal palaces of her father.

At first Huldbrand and Undine live most happily together; but ere long they meet an old lady-love of Huldbrand's, who sows dispeace. This maiden, Bertalda, has been brought up by a noble couple, but is, in reality, the child of the old people who reared Undine. Undine discovers this, and thinking to cause great joy, announces the fact. Bertalda is furious at her lowly parentage being proclaimed, and behaves so arrogantly that she disgusts her noble

*foster-parents by her conduct, and is turned out of doors by them. Undine
takes pity on her, and invites her to stay at Ringstetten, Huldbrand's castle.
There Huldbrand falls in love with Bertalda, and neglects his wife more and
more. Undine's kindred are ever on the watch to avenge her wrongs; but
their only mode of ingress is the castle well, and this Undine causes to be built
up. At last, on a sailing expedition, the knight, annoyed at the molestation
of Bertalda by the water-spirits, exclaims to Undine, in a burst of passion,
"Confine yourself to their company in the fiend's name, and do not longer
molest us human beings, juggling sorceress that you are!" Undine vanishes,
entreating her husband to remain faithful to her memory, that she may retain
the power of protecting him from injury. The knight, at first, feels remorse,
but erelong is consoled, and on the eve of marriage with Bertalda.*

Were I to offer a description of the nuptial festival at Castle
Ringstetten you would think you beheld a joyous show
covered with a pall of mourning—less a merry-making
than a satire on the nothingness of human joy. It was not
the fear of ghostly visitants, for they, as we know, had been
secured against by Undine's care. It was a curious gloom,
caused by the absence of the gracious lady who ought really
to have been presiding. Whenever a door opened, the
eyes of all involuntarily turned in that direction, and if it
chanced to be only a servant with a fresh supply of dainties,
or the cup-bearer with a draught of still more costly wine,
all again would look dejectedly to the ground, and the
spark of mirth and jollity that would sometimes appear,
were quickly extinguished in the falling tears of mournful
recollection. The bride was, of all, the most thoughtless,

and, consequently, the most contented. Yet, even to her, it appeared sometimes singular that she, with the wealth of myrtle and in richly embroidered attire, occupied the first place at the board, while Undine, stiff and cold, was lying on the ground of the Danube, or being borne by its current to the ocean.

Night was scarcely set in when the company dispersed— chased away by joyless depression and a boding sense of some impending evil. Bertalda retired with her maids, Huldbrand with his servants, to undress…

Bertalda was intent on rallying her spirits, and to this effect caused a rich casket of jewels Huldbrand had given her, together with rich dresses and veils, to be spread before her, in order to choose from them the gayest and most costly one to wear on the following day. Her maids were glad of the opportunity to say pleasing things to their young mistress, and more especially to praise her beauty in the brightest colours imaginable. They became more and more animated in these contemplations, till at last Bertalda, casting a look in the mirror, sighed: "Ah, but do you see how the sun has injured my complexion here at the side of my neck!" They looked, and found it was as their fair mistress had said, but they called it a beautiful mole that tended to enhance the whiteness of her skin. Bertalda shook her head, and was of opinion that it must still be considered a blemish. "And this," she said, sighing, "I might get rid of were not the castle well, from which I had such purifying water, unreasonably closed. If I had but a flask of it to-night."

"Is that all?" said one of her attendants, and disappeared from the chamber. "Surely," said Bertalda, agreeably surprised, "she will not take it into her head to have the stone removed this evening." But the tread of men was already heard across the court, and from the window she saw the complaisant waiting-maid leading them straight to the well, the levers and other implements they carried on their shoulders showing plainly enough what they were going to do.

"It is indeed my wish," said Bertalda, smiling, "if only it does not occupy them too long." And pleased at the thought that the least hint from her was now sufficient to obtain what formerly had been so sternly denied to her, she observed from her window the progress of their labour in the moonlit court.

The men pulled at the huge block, and one of them sighed, reflecting that they were destroying the work of their late mistress, who was still so dear to their remembrance.

But the matter was not nearly so difficult as they had expected. It was as though some power from within the well assisted them to remove the ponderous weight.

"One would imagine," said the workmen, "that the water was really mounting in the well."

The stone continued to rise, and with almost no exertion from the labourers, rolled, with a sullen sound, upon the pavement. But from the well a large column of water ascended with slow majestic motion, which, while they gazed, acquired the form and properties of a female figure clad in white, with a veil of the same colour depending from its head. It sobbed aloud, and clasped its hands with the most piteous action, and with lingering, unwilling steps, advanced towards the castle. The workmen fled terrified from the well, while the bride remained in horror at the window with her servants. When the figure came beneath her chamber, it looked upwards with melancholy gesture, and she seemed to recognise beneath the veil the features of Undine. Its gaze was but momentary; it passed on, yet slowly and reluctantly, as if dreading the limit of its travel. Bertalda called out to her attendants to wake Huldbrand, but not one dared to move from the spot, and even the bride herself was silent—alarmed by the very sound of her own voice.

While all stood thus at the window, motionless as statues, the strange wanderer had reached the castle gates. Onwards she went, up the well-known steps, through the familiar halls, always silent and always weeping. Alas! how different was her wandering through the castle once!

The knight had dismissed his servants—he stood half undressed before a large glass, with sad recollections of the past, and sadder forebodings of the future—the tapers burnt red and dim—there was a light tapping without upon the door as with a finger.

"It was thus," he whispered to himself, "Undine once used playfully to announce her coming, but it is all phantasy; I must to the wedding chamber."

"You must indeed, but into a dark and cold one," said a soft, thrilling voice.

As he looked in the glass he saw the door gently open—the figure in white entered—and the bolts of the lock shot back again into their fastenings.

"They have opened the well," it murmured; "and now I am here—and now you must die!"

His heart beat high, his breath came thick and short, he felt that it could not but be so; and covering his eyes, he exclaimed, "Make me not mad with terror in my dying hour—if you hide a countenance of terror beneath that veil, let me not see it—judge me without my looking on your face."

"Alas!" replied Undine, "will you not look on me yet once again? I am now as when you first saw me in the cottage."

"Oh, if it were so," sighed Huldbrand, "and I could die upon your bosom—in your kisses."

"It shall be so, my beloved," she replied, and her veil fell back, and she smiled in all her beauty. Trembling with love and the fear of approaching death, he bent towards her.

She kissed him with a heavenly kiss; but she loosed him no more from her embrace. She wept as she would weep away her soul. He dropped from her arms a lifeless corpse.

Undine, clad in white, and closely veiled, mingles with the funeral procession.

The last prayer was prayed, the last handful of earth was heaped upon the grave. They arose, and the stranger was no longer there, but where she had knelt a silver spring burst from the sward, that gently flowed and flowed till it surrounded the tomb.

THE MASQUE

When the Thirty Years' War was ravaging Germany, Klosterheim was ruled by
a Landgrave ostensibly on the side of the Imperialists, but secretly inclined to
the Swedes. He was a harsh and gloomy tyrant, suspected of dark crimes. The
town was packed with fugitives. Among these was the Lady Paulina, a relative
of the Emperor, and affianced, with his consent, to his protégé, the young
Maximilian. This was a youth of brilliant qualities and mysterious parentage,
who was pursuing his studies at Klosterheim University. Plots and counter-plots
were rife. The students were openly disaffected, and, by the Landgrave's orders,
were imprisoned in large numbers. After some time an order came for their
release. They were marched to the castle, headed by one of their ringleaders,
the Count St Aldenheim, and conducted before the Prince and his minister.

THIS PRINCE was now on the verge of fifty, strikingly
handsome in his features, and of imposing presence,
from the union of a fine person with manners unusually
dignified. No man understood better the art of restraining
his least governable impulses of anger or malignity within
the decorum of his rank. And even his worst passions,
throwing a gloomy rather than terrific air upon his features,

served less to alarm and revolt than to impress the sense of secret distrust. Of late indeed, from the too evident indications of the public hatred, his sallies of passion had become wilder and more ferocious, and his self-command less habitually conspicuous. But in general a gravity of insidious courtesy disguised from all but penetrating eyes the treacherous purpose of his heart.

The Landgrave bowed to the Count St Aldenhcim; and, pointing to a chair, begged him to understand that he wished to do nothing inconsistent with his regard for the Palsgrave his brother, and would be content with his parole of honour to pursue no further any conspiracy against himself, in which he might too thoughtlessly have engaged, and with his retirement from the city of Klosterheim.

The Count St Aldenheim replied that he and all the other cavaliers present, according to his belief, stood upon the same footing: that they had harboured no thought of conspiracy, unless that name could attach to a purpose of open expostulation with his Highness on the outraged privileges of their corporation as a university: that he wished not for any distinction of treatment in a case when all were equal offenders, or none at all: and, finally, that he believed the sentence of exile from Klosterheim would be cheerfully accepted by all, or most, of those present.

Adorni, the minister, shook his head, and glanced significantly at the Landgrave during this answer. The

Landgrave coldly replied that, if he could suppose the Count to speak sincerely, it was evident that he was little aware to what length his companions, or some of them, had pushed their plots. "Here are the proofs!" and he pointed to the papers.

"And now, gentlemen," said he, turning to the students, "I marvel that you, being cavaliers of family, and doubtless holding yourselves men of honour, should beguile these poor knaves into certain ruin, whilst yourselves could reap nothing but a brief mockery of the authority which you could not hope to evade."

Thus called upon, the students and the city-guard told their tale; in which no contradictions could be detected. The city prison was not particularly well secured against attacks from without. To prevent, therefore, any sudden attempt at a rescue, the guard kept watch by turns. One man watched two hours, traversing the different passages of the prison; and was then relieved. At three o'clock on the preceding night, pacing a winding lobby, brightly illuminated, the man who kept that watch was suddenly met by a person wearing a masque, and armed at all points. His surprise and consternation were great, and the more so as the steps of The Masque were soundless, though the floor was a stone one. The guard, but slightly prepared to meet an attack, would, however, have resisted or raised an alarm; but The Masque, instantly levelling a pistol at his head with one hand, with the other had thrown open the door of an empty cell, indicating to the man by signs that he must enter it. With this intimation he had necessarily complied; and The Masque had immediately turned the key upon him. Of what followed he knew nothing, until aroused by his comrades setting him at liberty, after some time had been wasted in searching for him.

The students had a pretty uniform tale to report. A Masque, armed *cap-a-pié* as described by the guard, had visited each of their cells in succession; had instructed them by signs to dress; and then, pointing to the door, by a series of directions all communicated in the same dumb show, had assembled them together, thrown open the prison door, and, pointing to their college, had motioned them thither. This motion they had seen no cause to disobey, presuming their dismissal to be according to the mode which best pleased his Highness, and not ill-pleased at finding so peaceful a termination to a summons which at first, from its mysterious shape and the solemn hour of night, they had understood as tending to some more formidable issue.

It was observed that neither the Landgrave nor his minister treated this report of so strange a transaction with the scorn which had been anticipated. Both listened attentively, and made minute inquiries as to every circumstance of the dress and appointments of the mysterious Masque. What was his height? By what road, or in what direction, had he disappeared? These questions answered, his Highness and his minister consulted a few minutes together, and then, turning to Von Aremberg, bade him for the present dismiss the prisoners to their homes,—an act of grace which seemed likely to do him service at the present crisis,—but at the same time to take sufficient security for their re-appearance. This done, the whole body were liberated.

All Klosterheim was confounded by the story of the mysterious Masque. For the story had been rapidly dispersed: and on the same day it was made known in another shape. A notice was affixed to the walls of several public places in these words:—

"Landgrave, beware! henceforth not you, but I, govern in Klosterheim. (Signed) "The Masque."

And this was no empty threat. Very soon it became apparent that some mysterious agency was really at work to counteract the Landgrave's designs. Sentinels were carried off from solitary posts. Guards even of a dozen men were silently trepanned from their stations. By and by, other attacks were made, even more alarming, upon domestic security. Was there a burgomaster amongst the citizens who had made himself conspicuously a tool of the Landgrave, or had opposed the Imperial interest? He was carried off in the night-time from his house, and probably from the city. At first this was an easy task. Nobody apprehending any special danger to himself, no special preparations were made to meet it. But, as it soon became apparent in what cause The Masque was moving, every person who knew himself obnoxious to attack took means to face it. Guards were multiplied; arms were repaired in every house; alarm bells were hung. For a time the danger seemed to diminish. The attacks were no longer so frequent. Still, wherever they were attempted, they succeeded just as before. It seemed, in fact, that all the precautions taken had no other effect than to warn The Masque of his own danger, and to place him more vigilantly on his guard. Aware of new defences rising, it seemed that he waited to see the course they would take; once master of that, he was ready (as it appeared) to contend with them as successfully as before.

Nothing could exceed the consternation of the city. Those even who did not fall within the apparent rule which governed the attacks of The Masque felt a sense of indefinite terror hanging over them. Sleep was no longer safe; the seclusion of a man's private hearth, the secrecy of bedrooms, was no longer a protection. Locks gave way, bars fell, doors flew open, as if by magic, before him. Arms seemed useless. In some instances a party of as many as ten or a dozen persons had been removed without rousing disturbance in the neighbourhood. Nor was this the only circumstance of mystery. Whither he could remove his victims was even more incomprehensible than the means by which he succeeded. All was darkness and fear; and the whole city was agitated with panic.

It began now to be suggested that a nightly guard should be established, having fixed stations or points of rendezvous, and at intervals parading the streets. This was cheerfully assented to; for, after the first week of the mysterious attacks, it began to be observed that the Imperial party were attacked indiscriminately with the Swedish. Many students publicly declared that they had been dogged through a street or two by an armed Masque; others had been suddenly confronted by him in unfrequented parts of the city in the dead of night, and were on the point of being attacked when some alarm, or the approach of distant footsteps, had caused him to disappear. The students, indeed, more particularly, seemed objects of attack; and, as they were pretty generally attached to the Imperial interest, the motives of The Masque were no longer judged to be political. Hence it happened that the students came forward in a body, and volunteered as members of the nightly guard. Being young, military for the most part in their habits, and trained to support the hardships of night-watching, they seemed peculiarly fitted for the service; and, as the case was no longer of a nature to awaken the suspicions of the Landgrave, they were generally accepted and enrolled, and with the more readiness as the known friends of the Prince came forward at the same time.

A night-watch was thus established, which promised security to the city, and a respite from their mysterious alarms. It was distributed into eight or ten divisions, posted at different points, whilst a central one traversed the whole city at stated periods, and overlooked the local stations. Such an arrangement was wholly unknown at that time in every part of Germany, and was hailed with general applause.

To the astonishment, however, of everybody, it proved wholly ineffectual. Houses were entered as before; the college chambers proved no sanctuary; indeed, they were attacked with a peculiar obstinacy, which was understood to express a spirit of retaliation for the alacrity of the students in combining for the public protection. People were carried off as before. And continual notices affixed to the gates of the college, the convents, or the schloss, with the signature of The Masque, announced to the public his determination to persist, and his contempt of the measures organised against him.

The alarm of the citizens now became greater than ever. The danger was one which courage could not face, nor prudence make provision for, nor wiliness evade. All alike, who had once been marked out for attack, sooner or later fell victims to the obstinacy of this mysterious foe. To have received even an individual warning availed them not at all. Sometimes it happened that, having received notice of suspicious circumstances indicating that The Masque had turned his attention upon themselves, they would assemble round their dwellings, or in their very chambers, a band of armed men sufficient to set the danger at defiance. But no sooner had they relaxed in these costly and troublesome arrangements, no sooner was the sense of peril lulled, and an opening made for their unrelenting enemy, than he glided in with his customary success; and in a morning or two after it was announced to the city that they also were numbered with his victims.

Even yet it seemed that something remained in reserve to augment the terrors of the citizens, and push them to excess. Hitherto there had been no reason to think that any murderous violence had occurred in the mysterious rencontres between The Masque and his victims. But of late, in those houses or college chambers from which the occupiers had disappeared, traces of bloodshed were apparent in some instances, and of ferocious conflict in others. Sometimes a profusion of hair was scattered on the ground; sometimes fragments of dress or splinters of weapons. Everything marked that on both sides, as this mysterious agency advanced, the passions increased in intensity; determination and murderous malignity on the one side, and the fury of resistance on the other.

At length the last consummation was given to the public panic; for, as if expressly to put an end to all doubts upon the spirit in which he conducted his warfare, in one house where the bloodshed had been so great as to argue some considerable loss of life, a notice was left behind in the following terms:—"Thus it is that I punish resistance; mercy to a cheerful submission; but henceforth death to the obstinate! The Masque."

What was to be done? Some counselled a public deprecation of his wrath, addressed to The Masque. But this, had it even offered any chance of succeeding, seemed too abject an act of abasement to become a large city. Under any circumstances, it was too humiliating a confession that, in a struggle with one man (for no more had avowedly appeared upon the scene), they were left defeated and at his mercy. A second party counselled a treaty. Would it not be possible to learn the ultimate objects of The Masque; and, if such as seemed capable of being entertained with honour, to concede to him his demands, in exchange for security to the city, and immunity from future molestation? It was true that no man knew where to seek him: personally he was hidden from their reach; but everybody knew how to find him: he was amongst them; in their very centre; and whatever they might address to him in a public notice would be sure of speedily reaching his eye.

After some deliberation, a summons was addressed to The Masque, and exposed on the college gates, and demanding of him a declaration of his purposes, and the price which he expected for suspending them. The next day an answer appeared in the same situation, avowing the intention of The Masque to come forward with ample explanation of his motives at a proper crisis, till which "more blood must flow in Klosterheim."

Meantime the Landgrave was himself perplexed and alarmed. Hitherto he had believed himself possessed of all the intrigues, plots, or conspiracies which threatened his influence in the city. Among the students and among the citizens he had many spies, who communicated to him whatsoever they could learn, which was sometimes more than the truth, and sometimes a good deal less. But now he was met by a terrific antagonist, who moved in darkness, careless of his power, inaccessible to his threats, and apparently as reckless as himself of the quality of his means.

Adorni, with all his Venetian subtlety, was now as much at fault as everybody else. In vain had they deliberated together, day after day, upon his probable purposes; in vain had they schemed to intercept his person, or offered high rewards for tracing his retreats. Snares had been laid for him in vain; every wile had proved abortive, every plot had been counterplotted. And both involuntarily confessed that they had now met with their master.

Vexed and confounded, fears for the future struggling with mortification for the past, the Landgrave was sitting, late at night, in the long gallery where he usually held his councils. He was reflecting with anxiety on the peculiarly unpropitious moment at which his new enemy had come upon the stage—the very crisis of the struggle between the Swedish and Imperial interests at Klosterheim, which would ultimately determine his own place and value in the estimate of his new allies. He was not of a character to be easily duped by mystery. Yet he could not but acknowledge to himself that there was something calculated to impress awe, and the sort of fear which is connected with the supernatural, in the sudden appearances, and vanishings as sudden, of The Masque. He came no one could guess whence, retreated no one could guess whither; was intercepted, and yet eluded arrest; and, if half the stories in circulation could be credited, seemed inaudible in his steps, at pleasure to make himself invisible and impalpable to the very hands stretched out to detain him. Much of this, no doubt, was wilful exaggeration, or the fictions of fears self-deluded. But enough remained, after every allowance, to justify an extraordinary interest in so singular a being; and the Landgrave could not avoid wishing that chance might offer an opportunity to himself of observing him.

Profound silence had for some time reigned throughout the castle. A clock which stood in the room broke it for a moment by striking the quarters; and, raising his eyes, the Landgrave perceived that it was past two. He rose to retire for the night, and stood for a moment musing with one hand resting upon the table. A momentary feeling of awe came across him, as his eyes travelled through the gloom at the lower end of the room, on the sudden thought—that a being so mysterious, and capable of piercing through so many impediments to the interior of every mansion in Klosterheim, was doubtless likely enough to visit the castle; nay, it would be no ways improbable that he should penetrate to this very room. What bars had yet been found sufficient to repel him? And who could pretend to calculate the hour of his visit? This night even might be the time which he would select. Thinking thus, the Landgrave was suddenly aware of a dusky figure entering the room by a door at the lower end. The room had the length and general proportions of a gallery, and the farther end was so remote from the candles which stood on the Landgrave's table that the deep gloom was but slightly penetrated by their rays. Light, however, there was, sufficient to display the outline of a figure slowly and inaudibly advancing up the room. It could not be said that the figure advanced stealthily; on the contrary, its motion, carriage, and bearing were in the highest degree dignified and solemn. But the feeling of a stealthy purpose was suggested by the perfect silence of its tread. The motion of a shadow could not be more noiseless. And this circumstance confirmed the Land-grave's first impression, that now he was on the point of accomplishing his recent wish, and meeting that mysterious being who was the object of so much awe, and the author of so far-spread a panic.

He was right; it was indeed The Masque, armed *cap-à-pié* as usual. He advanced with an equable and determined step in the direction of the Landgrave. Whether he saw His Highness, who stood a little in the shade of a large cabinet, could not be known; the Landgrave doubted not that he did. He was a prince of firm nerves by constitution, and of great intrepidity,—yet, as one who shared in the superstitions of his age, he could not be expected entirely to suppress an emotion of indefinite apprehension as he now beheld the solemn approach of a being who, by some unaccountable means, had trepanned so many different individuals from so many different houses, most of them prepared for self-defence, and fenced in by the protection of stone walls, locks, and bars.

The Landgrave, however, lost none of his presence of mind; and in the midst of his discomposure, as his eye fell upon the habiliments of this mysterious person, and the arms and military accoutrements which he bore, naturally his thoughts settled upon the more earthly means of annoyance which this martial apparition carried about him. The Landgrave was himself unarmed,—he had no arms even within reach,—nor was it possible for him in his present situation very speedily to summon assistance. With these thoughts passing rapidly through his mind, and sensible that, in any view of his nature and powers, the being now in his presence was a very formidable antagonist, the Landgrave could not but feel relieved from a burden of anxious tremors when he saw The Masque suddenly turn towards a door which opened about half-way up the room, and led into a picture-gallery at right angles with the room in which they both were.

Into the picture-gallery The Masque passed at the same solemn pace, without apparently looking at the Landgrave. This movement seemed to argue either that he purposely declined an interview with the Prince, and that might argue fear, or that he had not been aware of his presence;—either supposition, as implying something of human infirmity, seemed incompatible with supernatural faculties. Partly upon this consideration, and partly perhaps because he suddenly recollected that the road taken by The Masque would lead him directly past the apartments of the old seneschal, where assistance might be summoned, the Landgrave found his spirits at this moment revive. The consciousness of rank and birth also came to his aid, and that sort of disdain of the aggressor which possesses every man—brave or cowardly alike—within the walls of his own dwelling:—unarmed as he was, he determined to pursue, and perhaps to speak.

The restraints of high breeding, and the ceremonious decorum of his rank, involuntarily checked the Landgrave from pursuing with a hurried pace. He advanced with his habitual gravity of step, so that The Masque was half-way down the gallery before the Prince entered it. This gallery, furnished on each side with pictures, of which some were portraits, was of great length. The Masque and the Prince continued to advance, preserving a pretty equal distance. It did not appear by any sign or gesture that The Masque was aware of the Landgrave's pursuit. Suddenly, however, he paused—drew his sword—halted; the Landgrave also halted; then turning half round, and waving with his hand to the Prince so as to solicit his attention, slowly The Masque elevated the point of his sword to the level of a picture—it was the portrait of a young cavalier in a hunting dress, blooming with youth and youthful energy. The Landgrave turned pale, trembled, and was ruefully agitated. The Masque kept his sword in its position for half a minute; then dropping it, shook his head, and raised his hand with a peculiar solemnity of expression. The Landgrave recovered himself—his features swelled with passion—he quickened his step, and again followed in pursuit.

The Masque, however, had by this time turned out of the gallery into a passage which, after a single curve, terminated in the private room of the seneschal. Believing that his ignorance of the localities was thus leading him on to certain capture, the Landgrave pursued more leisurely.

The passage was dimly lighted; every image floated in a cloudy obscurity; and, upon reaching the curve, it seemed to the Landgrave that The Masque was just on the point of entering the seneschal's room. No other door was heard to open; and he felt assured that he had seen the lofty figure of The Masque gliding into that apartment. He again quickened his steps; a light burned within, the door stood ajar; quietly the Prince pushed it open, and entered with the fullest assurance that he should here at length overtake the object of his pursuit.

Great was his consternation upon finding in a room which presented no outlet not a living creature except the elderly seneschal, who lay quietly sleeping in his arm-chair. The first impulse of the Prince was to awaken him roughly, that he might summon aid and co-operate in the search. One glance at a paper upon the table arrested his hand. He saw a name written there, interesting to his fears beyond all others in the world. His eye was rivetted as by fascination to the paper. He read one instant. That satisfied him that the old seneschal must be overcome by no counterfeit slumbers, when he could thus surrender a secret of capital importance to the gaze of that eye from which above all others he must desire to screen it. One moment he deliberated with himself; the old man stirred, and muttered in his dreams; the Landgrave seized the paper, and stood irresolute for an instant whether to await his wakening, and authoritatively to claim what so nearly concerned his own interest, or to retreat with it from the room before the old man should be aware of the Prince's visit, or his own loss.

But the seneschal, wearied perhaps with some unusual exertion, had but moved in his chair; again he composed himself to deep slumber, made deeper by the warmth of a hot fire. The raving of the wind, as it whistled round this angle of the schloss, drowned all sounds that could have disturbed him. The Landgrave secreted the paper; nor did any sense of his rank and character interpose to check him in an act so unworthy of an honourable cavalier. Whatever crimes he had hitherto committed or authorised, this was perhaps the first instance in which he had offended by an instance of petty knavery. He retired with the stealthy pace of a robber anxious to evade detection; and stole back to his own apartments with an overpowering interest in the discovery he had made so accidentally, and with an anxiety to investigate it further, which absorbed for the time all other cares, and banished from his thoughts even The Masque himself, whose sudden appearance and retreat had in fact thrown into his hands the secret which now so exclusively disturbed him.

Meantime The Masque continued to harass the Landgrave, to baffle many of his wiles, and to neutralise his most politic schemes. In one of the many placards which he affixed to the castle gates, he described the Landgrave as ruling in Klosterheim by day, and himself by night. Sarcasms such as these, together with the practical insults which The Masque continually offered to the Landgrave by foiling his avowed designs, embittered the Prince's existence. The injury done to his political schemes of ambition at this particular crisis was irreparable. One after one, all the agents and tools by whom he could hope to work upon the counsels of the Klosterheim authorities, had been removed. Losing their influence, he had lost every prop of his own. Nor was this all: he was reproached by the general voice of the city as the original cause of a calamity which he had since shown himself impotent to redress. He it was, and his cause, which had drawn upon the people, so fatally trepanned, the hostility of the mysterious Masque. But for His Highness, all the burgomasters, captains, city officers, etc., would now be sleeping in their beds; whereas the best fate which could be surmised for the most of them was that they were sleeping in dungeons; some perhaps in their graves. And thus the Landgrave's cause not merely lost its most efficient partisans, but through their loss determined the wavering against him, alienated the few who remained of his own faction, and gave strength and encouragement to the general disaffection which had so long prevailed.

Thus it happened that the conspirators, or suspected conspirators, could not be brought to trial, or to punishment without a trial. Any spark of fresh irritation falling upon the present combustible temper of the populace would not fail to produce an explosion. Fresh conspirators, and real ones, were thus encouraged to arise. The university, the city, teemed with plots. The government of the Prince was exhausted with the growing labour of tracing and counteracting them. And, by little and little, matters came into such a condition that the control of the city, though still continuing in the Landgrave's hands, was maintained by mere martial force, and at the very point of the sword. And in no long time it was feared that with so general a principle of hatred to combine the populace, and so large a body of military students to head them, the balance of power, already approaching to an equipoise, would be turned against the Landgrave's government. And, in the best event, His Highness could now look for nothing from their love. All might be reckoned for lost that could not be extorted by force.

This state of things had been brought about by the dreadful Masque, seconded, no doubt, by those whom he had emboldened and aroused within; and, as the climax and crowning injury of the whole, every day unfolded more and more the vast importance which Klosterheim would soon possess as the centre and key of the movements to be anticipated in the coming campaign. An electoral cap would perhaps reward the services of the Landgrave in the general pacification, if he could present himself at the

German Diet as the possessor de facto of Klosterheim and her territorial dependencies, and with some imperfect possession de jure; still more, if he could plead the merit of having brought over this state, so important from local situation, as a willing ally to the Swedish interest. But to this a free vote of the city was an essential preliminary; and from that, through the machinations of The Masque, he was now farther than ever.

The temper of the Prince began to give way under these accumulated provocations. An enemy for ever aiming his blows with the deadliest effect; for ever stabbing in the dark; yet charmed and consecrated from all retaliation; always met with, never to be found! The Landgrave ground his teeth, clenched his fists, with spasms of fury. He quarrelled with his ministers; swore at the officers; cursed the sentinels; and the story went through Klosterheim that he had kicked Adorni.

Certain it was, under whatever stimulus, that Adorni put forth much more zeal at last for the apprehension of The Masque. Come what would, he publicly avowed that six days more should not elapse without the arrest of this "ruler of Klosterheim by night." He had a scheme for the purpose, a plot baited for snaring him; and he pledged his reputation as a minister and an intriguer upon its entire success.

On the following day, invitations were issued by Adorni, in His Highness's name, to a masqued ball on that day week. The fashion of masqued entertainments had been recently introduced from Italy into this sequestered nook of Germany; and here, as there, it had been abused to purposes of criminal intrigue.

Spite of the extreme unpopularity of the Landgrave with the low and middle classes of the city, among the highest his little court still continued to furnish a central resort to the rank and high blood, converged in such unusual proportion within the walls of Klosterheim. The schloss was still looked to as the standard and final court of appeal in all matters of taste, elegance, and high breeding. Hence it naturally happened that everybody with any claims to such an honour was anxious to receive a ticket of admission;—it became the test for ascertaining a person's pretensions to mix in the first circles of society; and, with this extraordinary zeal for obtaining an admission, naturally increased the minister's rigour and fastidiousness in pressing the usual investigation of the claimant's qualifications. Much offence was given on both sides, and many sneers hazarded at the minister himself, whose pretensions were supposed to be of the lowest description. But the result was that exactly twelve hundred cards were issued; these were regularly numbered, and below the device engraved upon the card was impressed a seal bearing the arms and motto of the Landgraves of X——— .

Every precaution was taken for carrying into effect the scheme, with all its details, as concerted by Adorni; and the third day of the following week was announced as the day of the expected fête.

The morning of the important day at length arrived, and all Klosterheim was filled with expectation. Even those who were not amongst the invited shared in the anxiety; for a great scene was looked for, and perhaps some tragical explosion. The undertaking of Adorni was known; it had been published abroad that he was solemnly pledged to effect the arrest of The Masque; and by many it was believed that he would so far succeed, at the least, as to bring on a public collision with that extraordinary personage. As to the issue, most people were doubtful, The Masque having hitherto so uniformly defeated the best-laid schemes for his apprehension. But it was hardly questioned that the public challenge offered to him by Adorni would succeed in bringing him before the public eye. This challenge had taken the shape of a public notice, posted up in the places where The Masque had usually affixed his own; and it was to the following effect:—"That the noble strangers now in Klosterheim, and others invited to the Landgrave's fête, who might otherwise feel anxiety in presenting themselves at the schloss, from an apprehension of meeting with the criminal disturber of the public peace, known by the appellation of The Masque, were requested by authority to lay aside all apprehensions of that nature, as the most energetic measures had been adopted to prevent or chastise upon the spot any such insufferable intrusion; and, for The Masque himself, if he presumed to disturb the company by his presence, he would be seized where he stood, and without further inquiry committed to the Provost-Marshal for instant execution;—on which account, all persons were warned carefully to forbear from intrusions of simple curiosity, since in the hurry of the moment it might be difficult to make the requisite distinctions."

It was anticipated that this insulting notice would not long go without an answer from The Masque. Accordingly, on the following morning, a placard, equally conspicuous, was posted up in the same public places, side by side with that to which it replied. It was couched in the following terms:—"That he who ruled by night in Klosterheim could not suppose himself to be excluded from a nocturnal fête given by any person in that city. That he must be allowed to believe himself invited by the Prince, and would certainly have the honour to accept His Highness's obliging summons. With regard to the low personalities addressed to himself, that he could not descend to notice anything of that nature coming from a man so abject as Adorni, until he should first have cleared himself from the imputation of having been a tailor in Venice at the time of the Spanish conspiracy in 1618, and banished from that city, not for any suspicions that could have settled upon him and his eight journeymen as making up one conspirator, but on account of some professional tricks in making a doublet for the Doge. For the rest, he repeated that he would not fail to meet the Landgrave and his honourable company."

All Klosterheim laughed at this public mortification offered to Adorni's pride; for that minister had incurred the public dislike as a foreigner, and their hatred on the score of private character. Adorni himself foamed at the mouth with rage, impotent for the present, but which he prepared to give deadly effect to at the proper time. But, whilst it laughed, Klosterheim also trembled. Some persons indeed were of opinion that the answer of The Masque was a mere sportive effusion of malice or pleasantry from the students, who had suffered so much by his annoyances. But the majority, amongst whom was Adorni himself, thought otherwise. Apart even from the reply, or the insult which had provoked it, the general impression was that The Masque would not have failed in attending a festival which, by the very costume which it imposed, offered so favourable a cloak to his own mysterious purposes. In this persuasion, Adorni took all the precautions which personal vengeance and Venetian subtlety could suggest, for availing himself of the single opportunity that would perhaps ever be allowed him for entrapping this public enemy, who had now become a private one to himself.

These various incidents had furnished abundant matter for conversation in Klosterheim, and had carried the public expectation to the highest pitch of anxiety, some time before the great evening arrived. Leisure had been allowed for fear, and every possible anticipation of the wildest character, to unfold themselves. Hope, even, amongst many, was a predominant sensation. Ladies were preparing for hysterics. Cavaliers, besides the swords which they wore as regular articles of dress, were providing themselves with stilettoes against any sudden rencontre hand to hand, or any unexpected surprise. Armourers and furbishers of weapons were as much in request as the more appropriate artists who minister to such festal occasions. These again were summoned to give their professional aid and attendance to an extent so much out of proportion to their numbers and their natural power of exertion that they were harassed beyond all physical capacity of endurance, and found their ingenuity more heavily taxed to find personal substitutes amongst the trades most closely connected with their own than in any of the contrivances which more properly fell within the business of their own art. Tailors, horse-milliners, shoemakers, friseurs, drapers, mercers, tradesmen of every description, and servants of every class and denomination, were summoned to a sleepless activity—each in his several vocation, or in some which he undertook by proxy. Artificers who had escaped on political motives from Nuremburg and other Imperial cities, or from the sack of Magdeburg, now showed their ingenuity, and their readiness to earn the bread of industry; and, if Klosterheim resembled a hive in the close-packed condition of its inhabitants, it was now seen that the resemblance held good hardly less in the industry which, upon a sufficient excitement, it was able to develop. But in the midst of all this stir, din, and unprecedented activity, whatever occupation each man found for his thoughts or for his hands in his separate employments, all hearts were mastered by one domineering interest—the approaching collision of the Landgrave, before his assembled court, with the mysterious agent who had so long troubled his repose.

The day at length arrived; the guards were posted in unusual strength: the pages of honour, and servants in their state-dresses, were drawn up in long and gorgeous files along the sides of the vast Gothic halls, which ran in continued succession from the front of the schloss to the more modern saloons in the rear; bands of military music, collected from amongst the foreign prisoners of various nations at Vienna, were stationed in their national costume—Italian, Hungarian, Turkish, or Croatian—in the lofty galleries or corridors which ran round the halls; and the deep thunders of the kettle-drums, relieved by cymbals and wind-instruments, began to fill the mazes of the palace as early as seven o'clock in the evening; for at that hour, according to the custom then established in Germany, such entertainments commenced. Repeated volleys from long lines of musketeers, drawn up in the square, and at the other entrances of the palace, with the deep roar of artillery, announced the arrival of the more distinguished visitors; amongst whom it was rumoured that several officers in supreme command from the Swedish camp, already collected in the neighbourhood, were this night coming incognito—availing themselves of their masques to visit the Landgrave and improve the terms of their alliance, whilst they declined the risk which they might have brought on themselves by too open a visit in their own avowed characters and persons to a town so unsettled in its state of feeling, and so friendly to the Emperor, as Klosterheim had notoriously become.

From seven to nine o'clock, in one unbroken line of succession, gorgeous parties streamed along through the halls, a distance of full half a quarter of a mile, until they were checked by the barriers erected at the entrance to the first of the entertaining rooms, as the station for examining the tickets of admission. This duty was fulfilled in a way which, though really rigorous in the extreme, gave no inhospitable annoyance to the visitors: the barriers themselves concealed their jealous purpose of hostility, and in a manner disavowed the secret awe and mysterious terror which brooded over the evening, by the beauty of their external appearance. They presented a triple line of gilt lattice-work, rising to a great altitude, and connected with a fretted roof by pendent draperies of the most magnificent velvet, intermingled with banners and heraldic trophies suspended from the ceiling, and at intervals slowly agitated in the currents which now and then swept these aerial heights. In the centre of the lattice opened a single gate, on each side of which were stationed a couple of sentinels armed to the teeth; and this arrangement was repeated three times, so rigorous was the vigilance employed. At the second of the gates, where the bearer of a forged ticket would have found himself in a sort of trap, with absolutely no possibility of escape, every individual of each successive party presented his card of admission, and, fortunately for the convenience of the company, in consequence of the particular precaution used, one moment's inspection sufficed. The cards had been issued to the parties invited not very long before the time of assembling; consequently as each was sealed with a private seal of the Landgrave's, sculptured elaborately with his armorial bearings, forgery would have been next to impossible.

These arrangements, however, were made rather to relieve the company from the too powerful terrors which haunted them, and to possess them from the first with a sense of security, than for the satisfaction of the Landgrave or his minister. They were sensible that The Masque had it in his power to command an access from the interior—and this it seemed next to impossible altogether to prevent; nor was that indeed the wish of Adorni, but rather to facilitate his admission, and afterwards, when satisfied of his actual presence, to bar up all possibility of retreat. Accordingly, the interior arrangements, though perfectly prepared, and ready to close up at the word of command, were for the present but negligently enforced.

Thus stood matters at nine o'clock, by which time upwards of a thousand persons had assembled; and in ten minutes more an officer reported that the whole twelve hundred were present without one defaulter.

The Landgrave had not yet appeared, his minister having received the company; nor was he expected to appear for an hour—in reality, he was occupied in political discussion with some of the illustrious incognitos. But this did not interfere with the progress of the festival; and at this moment nothing could be more impressive than the far-stretching splendours of the spectacle.

In one immense saloon, twelve hundred cavaliers and ladies, attired in the unrivalled pomp of that age, were arranging themselves for one of the magnificent Hungarian dances which the Emperor's court at Vienna had transplanted to the camp of Wallenstein, and thence to all the great houses of Germany. Bevies of noble women, in every variety of fanciful costume, but in each considerable group presenting deep masses of black or purple velvet, on which, with the most striking advantage of radiant relief, lay the costly pearl ornaments, or the sumptuous jewels, so generally significant in those times of high ancestral pretensions, intermingled with the drooping plumes of martial cavaliers, who presented almost universally the soldierly air of frankness which belongs to active service, mixed with the Castilian *grandezza* that still breathed through the camps of Germany, emanating originally from the magnificent courts of Brussels, of Madrid, and of Vienna, and propagated to this age by the links of Tilly, the Bavarian commander, and Wallenstein, the more than princely commander for the Emperor. Figures and habiliments so commanding were of themselves enough to fill the eye and occupy the imagination; but beyond all this, feelings of awe and mystery, under more shapes than one, brooded over the whole scene, and diffused a tone of suspense and intense excitement throughout the vast assembly. It was known that illustrious strangers were present incognito. There now began to be some reason for anticipating a great battle in the neighbourhood. The men were now present, perhaps the very hands were now visibly displayed for the coming dance which in a few days or even hours (so rapid were the movements at this period) were to wield the truncheon that might lay the Catholic empire prostrate, or might mould the destiny of Europe for centuries. Even this feeling gave way to one still more enveloped in shades. The Masque! Would he keep his promise and appear? might he not be there already? might he not even now be moving amongst them? may he not, even at this very moment, thought each person, secretly be near me—or even touching myself—or haunting my own steps?

Yet again, thought most people (for at that time hardly anybody affected to be incredulous in matters allied to the supernatural), was this mysterious being liable to touch? Was he not of some impassive nature, inaudible, invisible, impalpable? Many of his escapes, if truly reported, seemed to argue as much. If, then, connected with the spiritual world, was it with the good or the evil in that inscrutable region? But then the bloodshed, the torn dresses, the marks of deadly struggle, which remained behind in some of those cases where mysterious disappearances had occurred,— these seemed undeniable arguments of murder, foul and treacherous murder. Every attempt, in short, to penetrate the mystery of this being's nature proved as abortive as the attempts to intercept his person; and all efforts at applying a solution to the difficulties of the case made the mystery even more mysterious.

These thoughts, however, generally as they pervaded the company, would have given way for a time at least to the excitement of the scene; for a sudden clapping of hands from some officers of the household, to enforce attention, and as a signal to the orchestra in one of the galleries, at this moment proclaimed that the dances were on the point of commencing in another half minute, when suddenly a shriek from a female, and then a loud tumultuous cry from a multitude of voices, announced some fearful catastrophe; and in the next moment a shout of "Murder!" froze the blood of the timid amongst the company.

So vast was the saloon that it had been impossible through the maze of figures, the confusion of colours, and the mingling of a thousand voices, that anything should be perceived distinctly at the lower end of all that was now passing at the upper. Still, so awful is the mystery of life, and so hideous and accursed in man's imagination is every secret extinction of that consecrated lamp, that no news thrills so deeply, or travels so rapidly. Hardly could it be seen in what direction, or through whose communication, yet in less than a minute a movement of sympathising horror, and uplifted hands, announced that the dreadful news had reached them. A murder, it was said, had been committed in the palace. Ladies began to faint; others hastened away in search of friends; others to learn the news more accurately; and some of the gentlemen, who thought themselves sufficiently privileged by rank, hurried off with a stream of agitated inquiries to the interior of the castle, in search of the scene itself. A few only passed the guard in the first moments of confusion, and penetrated with the agitated Adorni through the long and winding passages, into the very scene of the murder. A rumour had prevailed for a moment that the Landgrave was himself the victim: and, as the road by which the agitated household conducted them took a direction towards his Highness's suite of rooms, at first Adorni had feared that result. Recovering his self-possession, however, at length he learned that it was the poor old seneschal upon whom the blow had fallen. And he pressed on with more coolness to the dreadful spectacle.

The poor old man was stretched at his length on the floor. It did not seem that he had struggled with the murderer. Indeed, from some appearances, it seemed probable that he had been attacked whilst sleeping; and, though he had received three wounds, it was pronounced by a surgeon that one of them (and that, from circumstances, the first) had been sufficient to extinguish life. He was discovered by his daughter, a woman who held some respectable place amongst the servants of the castle; and every presumption concurred in fixing the time of the dreadful scene to about one hour before.

"Such, gentlemen, are the acts of this atrocious monster, this Masque, who has so long been the scourge of Klosterheim," said Adorni to the strangers who had accompanied him, as they turned away on their return to the company; "but this very night, I trust, will put a bridle in his mouth."

"God grant it may be so!" said some. But others thought the whole case too mysterious for conjectures, and too solemn to be decided by presumptions. And in the midst of agitated discussions on the scene they had just witnessed, as well as the whole history of The Masque, the party returned to the saloon.

Under ordinary circumstances, this dreadful event would have damped the spirits of the company; as it was, it did but deepen the gloomy excitement which already had possession of all present, and raise a more intense expectation of the visit so publicly announced by The Masque. It seemed as though he had perpetrated this recent murder merely by way of reviving the impression of his own dreadful character in Klosterheim, which might have decayed a little of late, in all its original strength and freshness of novelty; or, as though he wished to send immediately before him an act of atrocity that should form an appropriate herald or harbinger of his own entrance upon the scene.

Dreadful, however, as this deed of darkness was, it seemed of too domestic a nature to exercise any continued influence upon so distinguished an assembly, so numerous, so splendid, and brought together at so distinguished a summons. Again, therefore, the masques prepared to mingle in the dance; again the signal was given; again the obedient orchestra preluded to the coming strains. In a moment more, the full tide of harmony swept along. The vast saloon, and its echoing roof, rang with the storm of music. The masques, with their floating plumes and jewelled caps, glided through the fine mazes of the Hungarian dances. All was one magnificent and tempestuous confusion overflowing with the luxury of sound and sight, when suddenly, about midnight, a trumpet sounded, the Landgrave entered, and all was hushed. The glittering crowd arranged themselves in a half circle at the upper end of the room; his Highness went rapidly round, saluting the company, and receiving their homage in return. A signal was again made; the music and the dancing were resumed; and such was the animation and the turbulent delight amongst the gayer part of the company, from the commingling of youthful blood with wine, lights, music, and festal conversation, that, with many, all thoughts of the dreadful Masque who "reigned by night in Klosterheim" had faded before the exhilaration of the moment. Midnight had come; the dreadful apparition had not yet entered: young ladies began timidly to jest upon the subject, though as yet but faintly, and in a tone somewhat serious for a jest; and young cavaliers, who, to do them justice, had derived most part of their terrors from the superstitious view of the case, protested to their partners that if The Masque, on making his appearance, should conduct himself in a manner unbecoming a cavalier, or offensive to the ladies present, they should feel it their duty to chastise him; "though," said they, "with respect to old Adorni, should The Masque think proper to teach him better manners, or even to cane him, we shall not find it necessary to interfere."

Several of the very young ladies protested that, of all things, they should like to see a battle between old Adorni and The Masque, "such a love of a quiz that old Adorni is!" whilst others debated whether The Masque would turn out a young man or an old one; and a few elderly maidens mooted the point whether he were likely to be a "single" gentleman, or burdened with a "wife and family." These and similar discussions were increasing in vivacity, and kindling more and more gaiety of repartee, when suddenly, with the effect of a funeral knell upon their mirth, a whisper began to circulate, that there was one masque too many in company. Persons had been stationed by Adorni in different galleries, with instructions to note accurately the dress of every person in the company; to watch the motions of every one who gave the slightest cause for suspicion, by standing aloof from the rest of the assembly, or by any other peculiarity of manner; but, above all, to count the numbers of the total assembly. This last injunction was more easily obeyed than at first sight seemed possible. At this time, the Hungarian dances, which required a certain number of partners to execute the movements of the figure, were of themselves a sufficient register of the precise amount of persons engaged in them. And, as these dances continued for a long time undisturbed, this calculation, once made, left no further computation necessary than simply to take the account of all who stood otherwise engaged. This list, being much the smaller one, was soon made; and the reports of several different observers, stationed in different galleries, and checked by each other, all tallied in reporting a total of just twelve hundred and one persons, after every allowance was made for the known members of the Landgrave's suite, who were all unmasked.

This report was announced, with considerable trepidation, in a very audible whisper to Adorni and the Landgrave. The buzz of agitation attracted instant attention; the whisper was loud enough to catch the ears of several; the news went rapidly kindling through the room that the company was too many by one: all the ladies trembled, their knees shook, their voices failed, they stopped in the very middle of questions, answers halted for their conclusion and were never more remembered by either party; the very music began to falter, the lights seemed to wane and sicken; for the fact was now too evident—that The Masque had kept his appointment, and was at this moment in the room, "to meet the Landgrave and his honourable company."

Adorni and the Landgrave now walked apart from the rest of the household, and were obviously consulting together on the next step to be taken, or on the proper moment for executing one which had already been decided on. Some crisis seemed approaching, and the knees of many ladies knocked together, as they anticipated some cruel or bloody act of vengeance. "Oh, poor Masque!" sighed a young lady in her tender-hearted concern for one who seemed now at the mercy of his enemies: "Do you think, sir," addressing her partner, "they will cut him to pieces?"— "Oh, that wicked old Adorni!" exclaimed another; "I know he will stick the poor Masque on one side, and somebody else will stick him on the other; I know he will, because The Masque called him a tailor: do you think he was a tailor, sir?"—"Why, really, madam, he walks like a tailor; but then he must be a very bad one, considering how ill his own clothes are made; and that, you know, is next door to being none at all. But see, his Highness is going to stop the music."

In fact, at that moment the Landgrave made a signal to the orchestra; the music ceased abruptly; and his Highness, advancing to the company, who stood eagerly awaiting his words, said—"Illustrious and noble friends! for a very urgent and special cause I will request of you all to take your seats."

The company obeyed: every one sought the chair next to him, or, if a lady, accepted that which was offered by the cavalier at her side. The standers continually diminished. Two hundred were left, one hundred and fifty, eighty, sixty, twenty, till at last they were reduced to two,—both gentlemen, who had been attending upon ladies. They were suddenly aware of their own situation. One chair only remained out of twelve hundred. Eager to exonerate himself from suspicion, each sprang furiously to this seat; each attained it at the same moment, and each possessed himself of part at the same instant. As they happened to be two elderly corpulent men, the younger cavaliers, under all the restraints of the moment, the panic of the company, and the Landgrave's presence, could not forbear laughing; and the more spirited amongst the young ladies caught the infection.

His Highness was little in a temper to brook this levity; and hastened to relieve the joint occupants of the chair from the ridicule of their situation. "Enough!" he exclaimed, "enough! all my friends are requested to resume the situation most agreeable to them; my purpose is answered."—The Prince was himself standing with all his household, and, as a point of respect, all the company rose. ("As you were," whispered the young soldiers to their fair companions.)

Adorni now came forward. "It is known," said he, "by trials more than sufficient, that some intruder, with the worst intentions, has crept into this honourable company. The ladies present will therefore have the goodness to retire apart to the lower end of the saloon, whilst the noble cavaliers will present themselves in succession to six officers of his Highness's household, to whom they will privately communicate their names and quality."

This arrangement was complied with, not, however, without the exchange of a few flying jests on the part of the young cavaliers and their fair partners, as they separated for the purpose. The cavaliers, who were rather more than five hundred in number, went up as they were summoned by the number marked upon their cards of admission, and, privately communicating with some one of the officers appointed, were soon told off, and filed away to the right of the Landgrave, waiting for the signal which should give them permission to rejoin their parties.

All had been now told off, within a score. These were clustered together in a group; and in that group undoubtedly was The Masque. Every eye was converged upon this small knot of cavaliers; each of the spectators, according to his fancy, selected the one who came nearest in dress, or in personal appearance, to his preconceptions of that mysterious agent. Not a word was uttered, not a whisper; hardly a robe was heard to rustle, or a feather to wave.

The twenty were rapidly reduced to twelve, these to six, the six to four—three—two; the tale of the invited was complete, and one man remained behind. That was, past doubting, The Masque.

"There stands he that governs Klosterheim by night!" thought every cavalier, as he endeavoured to pierce the gloomy being's concealment, with penetrating eyes, or by scrutiny ten times repeated, to unmasque the dismal secrets which lurked beneath his disguise. "There stands the gloomy murderer!" thought another. "There stands the poor detected criminal," thought the pitying young ladies, "who in the next moment must lay bare his breast to the Landgrave's musketeers."

The figure meantime stood tranquil and collected, apparently not in the least disturbed by the consciousness of his situation, or the breathless suspense of more than a thousand spectators of rank and eminent station, all bending their looks upon himself. He had been leaning against a marble column, as if wrapt up in reverie, and careless of everything about him. But, when the dead silence announced that the ceremony was closed, that he only remained to answer for himself, and upon palpable proof—evidence not to be gainsaid—incapable of answering satisfactorily; when, in fact, it was beyond dispute that here was at length revealed, in bodily presence, before the eyes of those whom he had so long haunted with terrors, The Masque of Klosterheim,—it was naturally expected that now at least he would show alarm and trepidation; that he would prepare for defence, or address himself to instant flight.

Far otherwise!—cooler than any one person beside in the saloon, he stood, like the marble column against which he had been reclining, upright—massy—and imperturbable. He was enveloped in a voluminous mantle, which at this moment, with a leisurely motion, he suffered to fall at his feet, and displayed a figure in which the grace of an

Antinous met with the columnar strength of a Grecian Hercules,—presenting, in its *tout ensemble*, the majestic proportions of a Jupiter. He stood—a breathing statue of gladiatorial beauty, towering above all who were near him, and eclipsing the noblest specimens of the human form which the martial assembly presented. A buzz of admiration arose, which in the following moment was suspended by the dubious recollections investing his past appearances, and the terror which waited even on his present movements. He was armed to the teeth; and he was obviously preparing to move.

Not a word had yet been spoken; so tumultuous was the succession of surprises, so mixed and conflicting the feelings, so intense the anxiety. The arrangement of the groups was this:—At the lower half of the room, but starting forward in attitudes of admiration or suspense, were the ladies of Klosterheim. At the upper end, in the centre, one hand raised to bespeak attention, was The Masque of Klosterheim. To his left, and a little behind him, with a subtle Venetian countenance, one hand waving back a half file of musketeers, and the other raised as if to arrest the arm of The Masque, was the wily minister Adorni—creeping nearer and nearer with a stealthy stride. To his right was the great body of Klosterheim cavaliers, a score of students and young officers pressing forward to the front; but in advance of the whole, the Landgrave of X——— , haughty, lowering, and throwing out looks of defiance. These were the positions and attitudes in which the first discovery of The Masque had surprised them; and these they still retained.

Less dignified spectators were looking downwards from the galleries.

"Surrender!" was the first word by which silence was broken; it came from the Landgrave.

"Or die!" exclaimed Adorni.

"He dies in any case," rejoined the Prince.

The Masque still raised his hand with the action of one who bespeaks attention. Adorni he deigned not to notice. Slightly inclining his head to the Landgrave, in a tone to which it might be the headdress of elaborate steelwork that gave a sepulchral tone, he replied,—

"The Masque, who rules in Klosterheim by night, surrenders not. He can die. But first he will complete the ceremony of the night, he will reveal himself."

"That is superfluous," exclaimed Adorni; "we need no further revelations. Seize him, and lead him out to death!"

"Dog of an Italian!" replied The Masque, drawing a dag from his belt, "die first yourself!" And so saying, he slowly turned and levelled the barrel at Adorni, who fled with two bounds to the soldiers in the rear. Then, withdrawing the weapon hastily, he added in a tone of cool contempt, "Or bridle that coward's tongue."

But this was not the minister's intention. "Seize him!" he cried again impetuously to the soldiers, laying his hand on the arm of the foremost, and pointing them forward to their prey.

"No!" said the Landgrave, with a commanding voice; "Halt! I bid you." Something there was in the tone, or it might be that there was something in his private recollections, or something in the general mystery, which promised a discovery that he feared to lose by the too precipitate vengeance of the Italian. "What is it, mysterious being, that you would reveal? Or who is it that you now believe interested in your revelations?"

"Yourself.—Prince, it would seem that you have me at your mercy: wherefore then the coward haste of this Venetian hound! I am one; you are many. Lead me then out; shoot me. But no: Freely I entered this hall; freely I will leave it. If I must die, I will die as a soldier. Such I am; and neither runagate from a foreign land; nor"—turning to Adorni—"a base mechanic."

"But a murderer!" shrieked Adorni: "but a murderer; and with hands yet reeking from innocent blood!"

"Blood, Adorni, that I will yet avenge.—Prince, you demand the nature of my revelations. I will reveal my name, my quality, and my mission."

"And to whom?"

"To yourself, and none beside. And, as a pledge for the

sincerity of my discoveries, I will first of all communicate a dreadful secret, known, as you fondly believe, to none but your Highness. Prince, dare you receive my revelations?"

Speaking thus, The Masque took one step to the rear, turning his back upon the room, and by a gesture signified his wish that the Landgrave should accompany him. But at this motion ten or a dozen of the foremost among the young cavaliers started forward in advance of the Land-grave, in part forming a half circle about his person, and in part commanding the open doorway.

"He is armed!" they exclaimed; "and trebly armed: will your Highness approach him too nearly?"

"I fear him not," said the Landgrave, with something of a contemptuous tone.

"Wherefore should you fear me?" retorted The Masque, with a manner so tranquil and serene as involuntarily to disarm suspicion. "Were it possible that I should seek the life of any man here in particular, in that case (pointing to the firearms in his belt), why should I need to come nearer? Were it possible that any should find in my conduct here a motive to a personal vengeance upon myself, which of you is not near enough? Has your Highness the courage to trample on such terrors?"

Thus challenged as it were to a trial of his courage before the assembled rank of Klosterheim, the Landgrave waved off all who would have stepped forward officiously to his support. If he felt any tremors, he was now sensible that pride and princely honour called upon him to dissemble them. And, probably, that sort of tremors which he felt in reality did not point in the direction to which physical support, such as was now tendered, could have been available. He hesitated no longer, but strode forward to meet The Masque. His Highness and The Masque met near the archway of the door, in the very centre of the groups.

With a thrilling tone, deep—piercing—full of alarm, The Masque began thus:—

"To win your confidence, for ever to establish credit with your Highness, I will first of all reveal the name of that murderer who this night dared to pollute your palace with an old man's blood. Prince, bend your ear a little this way."

With a shudder, and a visible effort of self-command, the Landgrave inclined his ear to The Masque, who added "Your Highness will be shocked to hear it": then in a lower tone, "Who could have believed it? It was ——" All was pronounced clearly and strongly, except the last word—the name of the murderer: that was made audible only to the Landgrave's ear.

Sudden and tremendous was the effect upon the Prince: he reeled a few paces off; put his hand to the hilt of his sword; smote his forehead; threw frenzied looks upon The Masque,—now half imploring, now dark with vindictive wrath. Then succeeded a pause of profoundest silence, during which all the twelve hundred visitors, whom he had himself assembled, as if expressly to make them witnesses of this extraordinary scene, and of the power with which a stranger could shake him to and fro in tempestuous strife of passions, were looking and hearkening with senses on the stretch to pierce the veil of silence and of distance. At last the Landgrave mastered his emotions sufficiently to say, "Well, sir, what next?"

"Next comes a revelation of another kind; and I warn you, sir, that it will not be less trying to the nerves. For this first I needed your ear; now I shall need your eyes. Think again, Prince, whether you will stand the trial."

"Pshaw! sir, you trifle with me; again I tell you——" But here the Landgrave spoke with an affectation of composure and with an effort that did not escape notice;—"again I tell you that I fear you not—Go on."

"Then come forward a little, please your Highness, to the light of this lamp." So saying, with a step or two in advance, he drew the Prince under the powerful glare of a lamp suspended near the great archway of entrance from the interior of the palace. Both were now standing with their faces entirely averted from the spectators. Still more effectually, however, to screen himself from any of those groups on the left whose advanced position gave them somewhat more the advantage of an oblique aspect, The Masque, at this moment, suddenly drew up, with his left hand, a short Spanish mantle which depended from his shoulders, and now gave him the benefit of a lateral screen. Then, so far as the company behind them could guess at his act, unlocking with his right hand and raising the masque which shrouded his mysterious features, he shouted aloud in a voice that rang clear through every corner of the vast saloon, "Landgrave, for crimes yet unrevealed, I summon you in twenty days, before a tribunal where there is no shield but innocence!" and at that moment turned his countenance full upon the Prince.

With a yell, rather than a human expression of terror, the Landgrave fell as if shot by a thunderbolt, stretched at his full length upon the ground, lifeless apparently, and bereft of consciousness or sensation. A sympathetic cry of horror arose from the spectators. All rushed towards The Masque. The young cavaliers who had first stepped forward as volunteers in the Landgrave's defence were foremost, and interposed between The Masque and the outstretched arms of Adorni, as if eager to seize him first. In an instant a sudden and dense cloud of smoke arose, nobody knew whence. Repeated discharges of firearms were heard resounding from the doorway and the passages; these increased the smoke and the confusion. Trumpets sounded through the corridors. The whole archway under which The Masque and the Landgrave had been standing became choked up with soldiery, summoned by the furious alarms that echoed through the palace. All was one uproar and chaos of masques, plumes, helmets, halberds, trumpets, gleaming sabres, and the fierce faces of soldiery forcing themselves through the floating drapery of smoke that now filled the whole upper end of the saloon. Adorni was seen in the midst, raving fruitlessly. Nobody heard: nobody listened. Universal panic had seized the household, the soldiery, and the company. Nobody understood exactly for what purpose the tumult had commenced—in what direction it tended. Some tragic catastrophe was reported from mouth to mouth: nobody knew what. Some said—the Landgrave had been assassinated; some—The Masque; some asserted that both had perished under reciprocal assaults. More believed that The Masque had proved to be of that supernatural order of beings with which the prevailing opinions of Klosterheim had long classed him; and that, upon raising his disguise, he had revealed to the Landgrave the fleshless skull of some forgotten tenant of the grave. This indeed seemed to many the only solution that, whilst it fell in with the prejudices and superstitions of the age, was of a nature to account for that tremendous effect which the discovery had produced upon the Landgrave. But it was one that naturally could be little calculated to calm the agitations of the public prevailing at this moment. This spread contagiously. The succession of alarming events, the murder, the appearance of The Masque, his subsequent extraordinary behaviour, the overwhelming impression upon the Landgrave, which had formed the catastrophe of this scenical exhibition,—the consternation of the great Swedish officers, who were spending the night in Klosterheim, and reasonably suspected that the tumult might be owing to the sudden detection of their own incognito, and that, in consequence, the populace of this Imperial city were suddenly rising to arms; the endless distraction and counteraction of so many thousand persons—visitors, servants, soldiery, household—all hurrying to the same point, and bringing assistance to a danger of which nobody knew the origin, nobody the nature, nobody the issue; multitudes commanding where all obedience was forgotten, all subordination had gone to wreck;—these circumstances of distraction united to sustain a scene of absolute frenzy in the castle, which, for more than half-an-hour, the dense columns of smoke aggravated alarmingly, by raising, in many quarters, additional terrors of fire. And when at last, after infinite exertions, the soldiery had deployed into the ball-room and the adjacent apartments of state, and had succeeded, at the point of the pike, in establishing a safe egress for the twelve hundred visitors, it was then first ascertained that all traces of The Masque had been lost in the smoke and subsequent confusion, and that, with his usual good fortune, he had succeeded in baffling his pursuers.

Paulina was, meanwhile, by means of forged letters, entrapped and carried off to a lonely castle, the residence of the Landgrave's innocent young daughter, who knew nothing of her father's crimes. Paulina was about to be tortured on account of her supposed connection with a conspiracy against the Landgrave, when she escaped from her gaolers and was succoured by her young hostess. The two maidens leave the castle together. The Landgrave, ignorant of his daughter's flight, issued orders for the female refugee to be shot without question when taken. Within the walls of Klosterheim, all is gloom and fear. The Landgrave relying on the growing power of the Swedes, becomes daily more tyrannous. To show his defiance of The Masque, and also as a cloak to his dark designs, he gives another great ball.

In twenty days the mysterious Masque had summoned the Landgrave "to answer, for crimes unatoned, before a tribunal where no power but that of innocence could avail him." These days were nearly expired. The morning of the Twentieth had arrived.

There were two interpretations of this summons. By many it was believed that the tribunal contemplated was that of the Emperor; and that, by some mysterious plot, which could not be more difficult of execution than others which had actually been accomplished by The Masque, on this day the Landgrave would be carried off to Vienna. Others, again, understanding by the tribunal, in the same sense, the Imperial chamber of criminal justice, believed it possible to fulfil the summons in some way less liable to delay or uncertainty than by a long journey to Vienna through a country beset with enemies. But a third party, differing from both the others, understood by the tribunal where innocence was the only shield—the judgment seat of heaven; and believed that on this day justice would be executed on the Landgrave, for crimes known and unknown, by a public and memorable death. Under any interpretation, however, nobody amongst the citizens could venture peremptorily to deny, after the issue of the masqued ball, and of so many other public denunciations, that The Masque would keep his word to the letter.

It followed of necessity that everybody was on the tip-toe of suspense, and that the interest hanging upon the issue of this night's events swallowed up all other anxieties, of whatsoever nature. Even the battle which was now daily expected between the Imperial and Swedish armies ceased to occupy the hearts and conversation of the citizens. Domestic and public concerns alike gave way to the coming catastrophe so solemnly denounced by The Masque.

The Landgrave alone maintained a gloomy reserve and the expression of a haughty disdain. He had resolved to meet the summons with the liveliest expression of defiance, by fixing this evening for a second masqued ball, upon a greater scale than the first. In doing this he acted advisedly, and with the counsel of his Swedish allies. They represented to him that the issue of the approaching battle might be relied upon as pretty nearly certain; all the indications were indeed generally thought to promise a decisive turn in their favour; but, in the worst case, no defeat of the Swedish army in this war had ever been complete; that the bulk of the retreating army, if the Swedes should be obliged to retreat, would take the road to Klosterheim, and would furnish to himself a garrison capable of holding the city for many months to come (and that would not fail to bring many fresh chances to all of them), whilst to his new and cordial allies this course would offer a secure retreat from pursuing enemies, and a satisfactory proof of his own fidelity. This even in the worst case; whereas, in the better and more probable one of a victory to the Swedes, to maintain the city but for a day or two longer against internal conspirators, and the secret co-operators outside, would be in effect to ratify any victory which the Swedes might gain by putting into their hands at a critical moment one of its most splendid trophies and guarantees.

These counsels fell too much into the Landgrave's own way of thinking to meet with any demurs from him. It was agreed, therefore, that as many Swedish troops as could at this important moment be spared should be introduced into the halls and saloons of the castle on the eventful evening, disguised as masquers. These were about four hundred; and other arrangements were made, equally mysterious, and some of them known only to the Landgrave.

At seven o'clock, as on the former occasion, the company began to assemble. The same rooms were thrown open; but, as the party was now far more numerous, and was made more comprehensive in point of rank, in order to include all who were involved in the conspiracy which had been for some time maturing in Klosterheim, fresh suites of rooms were judged necessary, on the pretext of giving fuller effect to the princely hospitalities of the Landgrave. And, on this occasion, according to an old privilege conceded in the case of coronations or galas of magnificence by the Lady Abbess of St Agnes, the partition walls were removed between the great hall of the schloss and the refectory of that immense convent; so that the two vast establishments, which on one side were contiguous to each other, were thus laid into one.

The company had now continued to pour in for two hours. The palace and the refectory of the convent were now overflowing with lights and splendid masques; the avenues and corridors rang with music; and, though every heart was throbbing with fear and suspense, no outward expression was wanting of joy and festal pleasure. For the present, all was calm around the slumbering volcano.

Suddenly the Count St Aldenheim, who was standing with arms folded, and surveying the brilliant scene, felt someone touch his hand, in the way concerted amongst the conspirators as a private signal of recognition. He turned, and recognised his friend, the Baron Adelort, who saluted him with three emphatic words—"We are betrayed!"— Then, after a pause, "Follow me."

St Aldenheim made his way through the glittering crowds, and pressed after his conductor into one of the most private corridors.

"Fear not," said the other, "that we shall be watched. Vigilance is no longer necessary to our crafty enemy. He has already triumphed. Every avenue of escape is barred and secured against us: every outlet of the palace is occupied by the Landgrave's troops. Not a man of us will return alive."

"Heaven forbid we should prove ourselves such gulls! You are but jesting, my friend."

"Would to God I were! my information is but too certain. Something I have overheard by accident; something has been told me; and something I have seen. Come you also, Count, and see what I will show you: then judge for yourself."

So saying, he led St Aldenheim by a little circuit of passages to a doorway, through which they passed into a hall of vast proportions: to judge by the catafalques and mural monuments, scattered at intervals along the vast expanse of its walls, this seemed to be the ante-chapel of St Agnes. In fact it was so; a few faint lights glimmered through the gloomy extent of this immense chamber, placed (according to the Catholic rite) at the shrine of the saint. Feeble as it was, however, the light was powerful enough to display in the centre a pile of scaffolding covered with black drapery.

Standing at the foot, they could trace the outlines of a stage at the summit, fenced in with a railing, a block, and the other apparatus for the solemnity of a public execution, whilst the sawdust below their feet ascertained the spot in which the heads were to fall.

"Shall we ascend and rehearse our parts?" asked the Count: "for methinks everything is prepared, except the headsman and the spectators. A plague on the inhospitable knave!"

"Yes, St Aldenheim, all is prepared—even to the sufferers. On that list, you stand foremost. Believe me, I speak with knowledge; no matter where gained. It is certain."

"Well, *necessitas non habet legem*; and he that dies on Tuesday will never catch cold on Wednesday. But still, that comfort is something of the coldest. Think you that none better could be had?"

"As how?"

"Revenge, *par exemple*; a little revenge. Might one not screw the neck of this base Prince, who abuses the confidence of cavaliers so perfidiously? To die I care not; but to be caught in a trap, and die like a rat lured by a bait of toasted cheese—Faugh! my countly blood rebels against it!"

"Something might surely be done, if we could muster in any strength. That is, we might die sword in hand; but——"

"Enough! I ask no more. Now, let us go. We will separately pace the rooms, draw together as many of our party as we can single out, and then proclaim ourselves. Let each answer for one victim. I'll take his Highness for my share."

With this purpose, and thus forewarned of the dreadful fate at hand, they left the gloomy ante-chapel, traversed the long suite of entertaining rooms, and collected as many as could easily be detached from the dances without too much pointing out their own motions to the attention of all present. The Count St Aldenheim was seen rapidly explaining to them the circumstances of their dreadful situation; whilst hands uplifted, or suddenly applied to the hilt of the sword, with other gestures of sudden emotion, expressed the different impressions of rage or fear which, under each variety of character, impressed the several hearers. Some of them, however, were too unguarded in their motions; and the energy of their gesticulations had now begun to attract the attention of the company.

The Landgrave himself had his eye upon him. But at this moment his attention was drawn off by an uproar of confusion in an antechamber, which argued some tragical importance in the cause that could prompt so sudden a disregard for the restraints of time and place. His Highness issued from the room in consternation, followed by many of the company. In the very centre of the anteroom, booted and spurred, bearing all the marks of extreme haste, panic, and confusion, stood a Swedish officer, dealing forth hasty fragments of some heart-shaking intelligence. "All is lost!" said he; "not a regiment has escaped!"

"And the place?" exclaimed a press of inquirers. "Nordlingen."

"And which way has the Swedish army retreated?" demanded a masque behind him.

"Retreat!" retorted the officer; "I tell you there is no retreat. All have perished. The army is no more. Horse, foot, artillery—all is wrecked, crushed, annihilated. Whatever yet lives is in the power of the Imperialists."

At this moment the Landgrave came up, and in every way strove to check these too liberal communications. He frowned; the officer saw him not. He laid his hand on the officer's arm, but all in vain. He spoke, but the officer knew not, or forgot his rank. Panic and immeasurable sorrow had crushed his heart; he cared not for restraints; decorum and ceremony were become idle words. The Swedish army had perished. The greatest disaster of the whole Thirty Years' War had fallen upon his countrymen. His own eyes had witnessed the tragedy, and he had no power to check or restrain that which made his heart overflow.

The Landgrave retired. But in half-an-hour the banquet was announced; and his Highness had so much command over his own feelings that he took his seat at the table. He seemed tranquil in the midst of general agitation; for the company were distracted by various passions. Some exulted in the great victory of the Imperialists, and the approaching liberation of Klosterheim. Some who were in the secret anticipated with horror the coming tragedy of vengeance upon his enemies which the Landgrave had prepared for this night. Some were filled with suspense and awe on the fulfilment in some way or other, doubtful as to the mode, but tragic (it was not doubted) for the result, of The Masque's mysterious denunciation.

Under such circumstances of universal agitation and suspense,—for on one side or other it seemed inevitable that this night must produce a tragical catastrophe,—it was not extraordinary that silence and embarrassment should at one moment take possession of the company, and at another that kind of forced and intermitting gaiety which still more forcibly proclaimed the trepidation which really mastered the spirits of the assemblage. The banquet was magnificent: but it moved heavily and in sadness. The music, which broke the silence at intervals, was animating and triumphant; but it had no power to disperse the gloom which hung over the evening, and which was gathering strength conspicuously as the hours advanced to midnight.

As the clock struck eleven, the orchestra had suddenly become silent; and, as no buzz of conversation succeeded, the anxiety of expectation became more painfully ir-ritating. The whole vast assemblage was hushed, gazing at the doors—at each other—or watching, stealthily, the Landgrave's countenance. Suddenly a sound was heard in an anteroom: a page entered with a step hurried and discomposed, advanced to the Landgrave's seat, and bending downwards, whispered some news or message to that Prince, of which not a syllable could be caught by the company. Whatever was its import, it could not be collected, from any very marked change on the features of him to whom it was addressed, that he participated in the emotions of the messenger, which were obviously those of grief or panic—perhaps of both united. Some even fancied that a transient expression of malignant exultation crossed the Landgrave's countenance at this moment. But, if that were so, it was banished as suddenly; and, in the next instant the Prince arose with a leisurely motion; and, with a very successful affectation (if such it were) of extreme tranquillity, he moved forwards to one of the anterooms, in which, as it now appeared, some person was awaiting his presence.

Who, and on what errand?—These were the questions which now racked the curiosity of those among the company who had least concern in the final event, and more painfully interested others whose fate was consciously dependent upon the accidents which the next hour might happen to bring up. Silence still continuing to prevail, and, if possible deeper silence than before, it was inevitable that all the company—those even whose honourable temper would least have brooked any settled purpose of surprising the Landgrave's secrets—should, in some measure, become a party to what was now passing in the anteroom.

The voice of the Landgrave was heard at times—briefly and somewhat sternly in reply—but apparently in the tone of one who is thrown upon the necessity of self-defence. On the other side, the speaker was earnest, solemn, and (as it seemed) upon an office of menace or upbraiding. For a time, however, the tones were low and subdued; but, as the passion of the scene advanced, less restraint was observed on both sides; and at length many believed that in the stranger's voice they recognised that of the Lady Abbess; and it was some corroboration of this conjecture that the name of Paulina began now frequently to be caught, and in connection with ominous words, indicating some dreadful fate supposed to have befallen her.

A few moments dispersed all doubts. The tones of bitter and angry reproach rose louder than before; they were without doubt those of the Abbess. She charged the blood of Paulina upon the Landgrave's head; denounced the instant vengeance of the Emperor for so great an atrocity; and, if that could be evaded, bade him expect certain retribution from Heaven for so wanton and useless an effusion of innocent blood.

The Landgrave replied in a lower key; and his words were few and rapid. That they were words of fierce recrimination was easily collected from the tone; and in the next minute the parties separated, with little ceremony (as was sufficiently evident) on either side, and with mutual wrath. The Landgrave re-entered the banqueting-room—his features discomposed and inflated with passion; but such was his self-command, and so habitual his dissimulation, that, by the time he reached his seat, all traces of agitation had disappeared; his countenance had resumed its usual expression of stern serenity, and his manners their usual air of perfect self-possession.

The clock of St Agnes struck twelve. At that sound the Landgrave rose. "Friends and illustrious strangers!" said he, "I have caused one seat to be left empty for that blood-stained Masque who summoned me to answer on this night for a crime which he could not name, at a bar which no man knows. His summons you heard. Its fulfilment is yet to come. But I suppose few of us are weak enough to expect——"

"That The Masque of Klosterheim will ever break his engagements," said a deep voice, suddenly interrupting the Landgrave. All eyes were directed to the sound; and behold! there stood The Masque, and seated himself quietly in the chair which had been left vacant for his reception.

"It is well!" said the Landgrave; but the air of vexation and panic with which he sank back into his seat belied his words. Rising again, after a pause, with some agitation he said, "Audacious criminal! since last we met, I have learned to know you, and to appreciate your purposes. It is now fit they should be known to Klosterheim. A scene of justice awaits you at present, which will teach this city to understand the delusions which could build any part of her hopes upon yourself.—Citizens and friends, not I, but these dark criminals and interlopers whom you will presently see revealed in their true colours, are answerable for that interruption to the course of our peaceful festivities which will presently be brought before you. Not I, but they are responsible."

So saying, the Landgrave arose, and the whole of the immense audience, who now resumed their masques, and prepared to follow whither his Highness should lead. With the haste of one who fears he may be anticipated in his purpose, and the fury of some bird of prey apprehending that his struggling victim may be yet torn from his talons, the Prince hurried onwards to the ante-chapel. Innumerable torches now illuminated its darkness; in other respects it remained as St Aldenheim had left it.

The Swedish masques had many of them withdrawn from the gala on hearing the dreadful day of Nordlingen. But enough remained, when strengthened by the bodyguard of the Landgrave, to make up a corps of nearly five hundred men. Under the command of Colonel Von Aremberg, part of them now enclosed the scaffold, and part prepared to seize the persons who were pointed out to them as conspirators. Amongst these stood foremost The Masque.

Shaking off those who attempted to lay hands upon him, he strode disdainfully within the ring; and then turning to the Landgrave he said—

"Prince, for once be generous; accept me as a ransom for the rest."

The Landgrave smiled sarcastically. "That were an unequal bargain, methinks, to take a part in exchange for the whole."

"The whole? And where is then your assurance of the whole?"

"Who should now make it doubtful? There is the block; the headsman is at hand. What hand can deliver from this extremity even you, Sir Masque?"

"That which has many times delivered me from a greater. It seems, Prince, that you forget the last days in the history of Klosterheim. He that rules by night in Klosterheim may well expect a greater favour than this when he descends to sue for it."

The Landgrave smiled contemptuously. "But again I ask you, sir, will you on any terms grant immunity to these young men?"

"You sue as vainly for others as you would do for yourself."

"Then all grace is hopeless?" The Landgrave vouchsafed no answer, but made signals to Von Aremberg.

"Gentlemen, cavaliers, citizens of Klosterheim, you that are not involved in the Landgrave's suspicions," said The Masque appealingly, "will you not join me in the intercession I offer for these young friends, who are else to perish unjudged, by blank edict of martial law?"

The citizens of Klosterheim interceded with ineffectual supplication.

"Gentlemen, you waste your breath; they die without reprieve," replied the Landgrave.

"Will your Highness spare none?"

"Not one," he exclaimed angrily, "not the youngest amongst them."

"Nor grant a day's respite to him who may appear on examination the least criminal of the whole?"

"A day's respite? No, nor half-an-hour's.—Headsman, be ready.—Soldiers, lay the heads of the prisoners ready for the axe."

"Detested Prince, now look to your own!"

With a succession of passions flying over his face, rage, disdain, suspicion, the Landgrave looked round upon The Masque as he uttered these words, and with pallid, ghastly consternation, beheld him raise to his lips a hunting horn which depended from his neck. He blew a blast, which was immediately answered from within. Silence as of the grave ensued. All eyes were turned in the direction of the answer. Expectation was at its summit; and in less than a minute solemnly uprose the curtain which divided the chapel from the ante-chapel, revealing a scene that smote many hearts with awe, and the consciences of some with as much horror as if it had really been that final tribunal which numbers believed The Masque to have denounced.

The great chapel of St Agnes, the immemorial hall of coronation for the Landgraves of X——— , was capable of containing with ease from seven to eight thousand spectators. Nearly that number was now collected in the galleries, which, on the recurrence of that great occasion, or of a royal marriage, were usually assigned to the spectators. These were all equipped in burnished arms, the very *élite* of the Imperial army. Resistance was hopeless; in a single moment the Landgrave saw himself dispossessed of all his hopes by an overwhelming force, the advanced guard in fact of the victorious Imperialists, now fresh from Nordlingen.

On the marble area of the chapel, level with their own position, were arranged a brilliant staff of officers; and a little in advance of them, so as almost to reach the ante-chapel, stood the Imperial Legate or Ambassador. This nobleman advanced to the crowd of Klosterheimers, and spoke thus:—

"Citizens of Klosterheim, I bring you from the Emperor your true and lawful Landgrave, Maximilian, son of your last beloved Prince."

Both chapels resounded with acclamations; and the troops presented arms.

"Show us our Prince! let us pay him our homage!" echoed from every mouth.

"This is mere treason!" exclaimed the Usurper. "The Emperor invites treason against his own throne who undermines that of other Princes. The late Landgrave had no son; so much is known to you all."

"None that was known to his murderer," replied The Masque; "else had he met no better fate than his unhappy father."

"Murderer!—And what art thou, blood-polluted Masque, with hands yet reeking from the blood of all who refused to join the conspiracy against your lawful Prince?"

"Citizens of Klosterheim," said the Legate, "first let the Emperor's friend be assoiled from all injurious thoughts. Those whom ye believe to have been removed by murder are here to speak for themselves."

Upon this the whole line of those who had mysteriously disappeared from Klosterheim presented themselves to the welcome of their astonished friends.

"These," said the Legate, "quitted Klosterheim, even by the same secret passages which enabled us to enter it, and for the self-same purpose,—to prepare the path for the restoration of the true heir, Maximilian the Fourth, whom in this noble Prince you behold, and whom may God long preserve!"

Saying this, to the wonder of the whole assembly he led forward The Masque, whom nobody had yet suspected for more than an agent of the true heir.

The Landgrave meantime, thus suddenly denounced as a tyrant—usurper—murderer, had stood aloof, and had given but a slight attention to the latter words of the Legate. A race of passions had traversed his countenance, chasing each other in flying succession. But by a prodigious effort he recalled himself to the scene before him; and striding up to the crowd, of which the Legate was the central figure, he raised his arm with a gesture of indignation, and protested vehemently that the assassination of Maximilian's father had been iniquitously charged upon himself:—"And yet," said he, "upon that one gratuitous assumption have been built all the other foul suspicions directed against my person."

"Pardon me, sir," replied the Legate, "the evidences were such as satisfied the Emperor and his Council; and he showed it by the vigilance with which he watched over the Prince Maximilian, and the anxiety with which he kept him from approaching your Highness until his pretensions could be established by arms. But, if more direct evidence were wanting, since yesterday we have had it in the dying confession of the very agent employed to strike the fatal blow. That man died last night penitent and contrite, having fully unburdened his conscience, at Waldenhausen.

With evidence so overwhelming, the Emperor exacts no further sacrifice from your Highness than that of retirement from public life, to any one of your own castles in your patrimonial principality of Oberhornstein.—But now for a more pleasing duty. Citizens of Klosterheim welcome your young Landgrave in the Emperor's name: and to-morrow you shall welcome also your future Landgravine, the lovely Countess Paulina, cousin to the Emperor, my master, and cousin also to your noble young Landgrave."

"No!" exclaimed the malignant usurper, "her you shall never see alive: for that, be well assured, I have taken care."

"Vile, unworthy Prince!" replied Maximilian, his eyes kindling with passion, "know that your intentions, so worthy of a fiend, towards that most innocent of ladies, have been confounded and brought to nothing by your own gentle daughter, worthy of a far nobler father."

"If you speak of my directions for administering the torture, a matter in which I presume that I exercised no unusual privilege amongst German sovereigns, you are right But it was not that of which I spoke."

"Of what else then?—The Lady Paulina has escaped."

"True, to Falkenberg. But, doubtless, young Landgrave, you have heard of such a thing as the intercepting of a fugitive prisoner; in such a case you know the punishment which martial law awards. The governor at Falkenberg had his orders." These last significant words he uttered in a tone of peculiar meaning. His eyes sparkled with bright gleams of malice and of savage vengeance, rioting in its completion.

"Oh, heart—heart!" exclaimed Maximilian, "can this be possible?"

The Imperial Legate and all present crowded around him to suggest such consolation as they could. Some offered to ride off express to Falkenberg; some argued that the Lady Paulina had been seen within the last hour. But the hellish exulter in ruined happiness destroyed that hope as soon as it dawned:—

"Children!" he said, "foolish children! cherish not such chimeras. Me you have destroyed, Landgrave, and the prospects of my house. Now perish yourself.—Look there: is that the form of one who lives and breathes?"

All present turned to the scaffold, in which direction he pointed, and now first remarked, covered with a black pall, and brought hither doubtless to aggravate the pangs of death to Maximilian, what seemed but too certainly a female corpse. The stature, the fine swell of the bust, the rich outline of the form, all pointed the same conclusion; and in this recumbent attitude, it seemed but too clearly to present the magnificent proportions of Paulina.

There was a dead silence. Who could endure to break it?

Who make the effort which was for ever to fix the fate of Maximilian?

He himself could not. At last the deposed usurper, craving for the consummation of his vengeance, himself strode forward; with one savage grasp he tore away the pall, and below it lay the innocent features, sleeping in her last tranquil slumber, of his own gentle-minded daughter!

No heart was found savage enough to exult—the sorrow even of such a father was sacred. Death, and through his own orders, had struck the only being whom he had ever loved; and the petrific mace of the fell destroyer seemed to have smitten his own heart and withered its hopes for ever.

Everybody comprehended the mistake in a moment. Paulina had lingered at Waldenhausen under the protection of an Imperial corps, which she had met in her flight. The tyrant, who had heard of her escape, but apprehended no necessity for such a step on the part of his daughter, had issued sudden orders to the officer commanding the military post at Falkenberg, to seize and shoot the female prisoner escaping from confinement, without allowing any explanations whatsoever, on her arrival at Falkenberg. This precaution he had adopted in part to intercept any denunciation of the Emperor's vengeance which Paulina might address to the officer. As a rude soldier, accustomed to obey the letter of his orders, this commandant had executed his commission; and the gentle Adeline, who had

274

naturally hastened to the protection of her father's chateau, surrendered her breath meekly and with resignation to what she believed a simple act of military violence; and this she did before she could know a syllable of her father's guilt or his fall, and without any the least reason for supposing him connected with the occasion of her early death.

At this moment Paulina made her appearance unexpectedly, to re-assure the young Landgrave by her presence, and to weep over her young friend, whom she had lost almost before she had come to know her. The scaffold, the corpse, and the other images of sorrow, were then withdrawn;—seven thousand Imperial troops presented arms to the youthful Landgrave and the future Landgravine, the brilliant favourites of the Emperor;—the immense area of St Agnes resounded with the congratulations of Klosterheim;—and as the magnificent cortege moved off to the interior of the schloss, the swell of the Coronation anthem rising in peals upon the ear from the choir of St Agnes, and from the military bands of the Imperial troops, awoke the promise of happier days, and of more equitable government, to the long-harassed inhabitants of Klosterheim.

The Klosterheimers knew enough already, personally or by questions easily answered in every quarter, to supply any links which were wanting in the rapid explanations of the Legate. Nevertheless, that nothing might remain liable to misapprehension or cavil, a short manifesto was this night circulated by the new government, from which the following facts are abstracted:—

The last rightful Landgrave, whilst yet a young man, had been assassinated in the forest when hunting. A year or two before this catastrophe he had contracted what, from the circumstances, was presumed at the time to be morganatic, or left-handed, marriage with a lady of high birth, nearly connected with the Imperial House. The effect of such a marriage went to incapacitate the children who might be born under it, male or female, from succeeding. On that account, as well as because current report had represented her as childless, the widow lady escaped all attempts from the assassin. Meantime this lady, who was no other than Sister Madeline, had been thus indebted for her safety to two rumours which were in fact equally false. She soon found means of convincing the Emperor, who had been the bosom friend of her princely husband, that her marriage was a perfect one, and conferred the fullest rights of succession upon her infant son Maximilian, whom at the earliest age, and with the utmost secrecy, she had committed to the care of his Imperial Majesty. This powerful guardian had in every way watched over the interests of the young prince. But the Thirty Years' War had thrown all Germany into distractions, which for a time thwarted the Emperor, and favoured the views of the usurper. Latterly also another question had arisen on the city and dependencies of Klosterheim as distinct from the Landgraviate. These, it was now affirmed, were a female appanage, and could only pass back to the Landgraves of X—— through a marriage with the female inheritrix. To reconcile all claims, therefore, on finding this bar in the way, the Emperor had resolved to promote a marriage for Maximilian with Paulina, who stood equally related to the Imperial house and to that of her lover. In this view he had despatched Paulina to Klosterheim, with proper documents to support the claims of both parties. Of these documents she had been robbed at Waldenhausen; and the very letter which was designed to introduce Maximilian as "the child and sole representative of the late murdered Landgrave," falling in this surreptitious way into the usurper's hand, had naturally misdirected his attacks to the person of Paulina.

For the rest, as regarded the mysterious movements of The Masque, these were easily explained. Fear, and the exaggerations of fear, had done one half the work to his hands, by preparing people to fall easy dupes to the plans laid, and by increasing the romantic wonders of his achievements. Co-operation also on the part of the very students and others who stood forward as the night watch for detecting him, had served The Masque no less powerfully. The appearances of deadly struggles had been arranged artificially to countenance the plot and to aid the terror. Finally, the secret passages which communicated between the forest and the chapel of St Agnes (passages of which many were actually applied to that very use in the Thirty Years' War) had been unreservedly placed at their disposal by the Lady Abbess, an early friend of the unhappy Landgravine, who sympathised deeply with that lady's unmerited sufferings.

One other explanation followed, communicated in a letter from Maximilian to the Legate; this related to the murder of the old seneschal, a matter in which the young Prince took some blame to himself—as having unintentionally drawn upon that excellent servant his unhappy fate. "The seneschal," said the writer, "was the faithful friend of my family, and knew the whole course of its misfortunes. He continued his abode at the schloss to serve my interest; and in some measure I may fear that I drew upon him his fate. Traversing late one evening a suite of rooms, which his assistance and my own mysterious disguise laid open to my passage at all hours, I came suddenly upon the Prince's retirement. He pursued me, but with hesitation. Some check I gave to his motions by halting before a portrait of my unhappy father, and emphatically pointing his attention to it. Conscience, I well knew, would supply a commentary to my act. I produced the impression which I had anticipated, but not so strongly as to stop his pursuit. My course necessarily drew him into the seneschal's room. The old man was sleeping; and this accident threw into the Prince's hands a paper, which, I have reason to think, shed some considerable light upon my own pretensions, and, in fact, first made my enemy acquainted with my existence and my claims. Meantime, the seneschal had secured the Prince's vengeance upon himself. He was now known as a faithful agent in my service. That fact signed his death-warrant. There is a window in a gallery which commands the interior of the seneschal's room. On the evening of the last fête, waiting there for an opportunity of speaking securely with this faithful servant, I heard a deep groan, and then another, and another; I raised myself, and with an ejaculation of horror, looked down upon the murderer—then surveying his victim with hellish triumph. My loud exclamation drew the murderer's eye upwards: under the pangs of an agitated conscience, I have reason to think that he took me for my unhappy father, who perished at my age, and is said to have resembled me closely. Who that murderer was, I need not say more directly. He fled with the terror of one who flies from an apparition. Taking a lesson from this incident, on that same night, by the very same sudden revelation of what passed, no doubt, for my father's countenance, aided by my mysterious character, and the proof I had announced to him immediately before of my acquaintance with the secret of the seneschal's murder—in this and no other way it was that I produced that powerful impression upon the Prince which terminated the festivities of that evening, and which all Klosterheim witnessed. If not, it is for the Prince to explain in what other way I did or could affect him so powerfully."

This explanation of the else unaccountable horror manifested by the ex-Landgrave on the sudden exposure of The Masque's features, received a remarkable confirmation from the confession of the miserable assassin at Waldenhausen. This man's illness had been first brought on by the sudden shock of a situation pretty nearly the same, acting on a conscience more disturbed and a more superstitious mind. In the very act of attempting to assassinate or rob Maximilian, he had been suddenly dragged by that Prince into a dazzling light; and this, settling full upon the features which too vividly recalled to the murderer's recollection that the last unhappy Landgrave at the very same period of blooming manhood, and in his own favourite hunting palace, not far from which the murder had been perpetrated, naturally enough had for a time unsettled the guilty man's understanding, and, terminating in a nervous fever, had at length produced his penitential death.

A death, happily of the same character, soon overtook the deposed Landgrave. He was laid by the side of his daughter, whose memory, as much even as his own penitence, availed to gather round his final resting-place the forgiving thoughts even of those who had suffered most from his crimes. Klosterheim in the next age flourished greatly, being one of those cities which benefited by the Peace of Westphalia. Many changes took place in consequence, greatly affecting the architectural character of the town and its picturesque antiquities; but, amidst all revolutions of this nature, the secret passages still survive,—and to this day are shown occasionally to strangers of rank and consideration,—by which, more than by any other of the advantages at his disposal, The Masque of Klosterheim was enabled to replace himself in his patrimonial rights, and at the same time to liberate from a growing oppression his own compatriots and subjects.